HARD WINTER

This Large Print Book carries the
Seal of Approval of N.A.V.H.

HARD WINTER

A WESTERN STORY

JOHNNY D. BOGGS

THORNDIKE PRESS
A part of Gale, Cengage Learning

GALE
CENGAGE Learning™

Detroit • New York • San Francisco • New Haven, Conn • Waterville, Maine • London

GALE
CENGAGE Learning™

Copyright © 2009 by Johnny D. Boggs.
Thorndike Press, a part of Gale, Cengage Learning.

ALL RIGHTS RESERVED
Thorndike Press® Large Print Western.
The text of this Large Print edition is unabridged.
Other aspects of the book may vary from the original edition.
Set in 16 pt. Plantin.
Printed on permanent paper.

LIBRARY OF CONGRESS CATALOGING-IN-PUBLICATION DATA

Boggs, Johnny D.
    Hard winter : a western story / by Johnny D. Boggs.
      p. cm. — (Thorndike Press large print western)
    ISBN-13: 978-1-4104-2353-5 (alk. paper)
    ISBN-10: 1-4104-2353-0 (alk. paper)
    1. Winter—Fiction. 2. Large type books. I. Title.
PS3552.O4375H366 2010
813'.54—dc22
                                      2009049088

Published in 2010 by arrangement with Golden West Literary Agency.

Printed in the United States of America
1 2 3 4 5 6 7 14 13 12 11 10 —

For Ol' Max Evans
Pardner, I can never thank you enough.

Spring, 1920
A little bird told John Burroughs, the naturalist, it's to be a long, hard winter.
— *Kansas City Star,*
December 13, 1919

CHAPTER ONE

Weather and creaking joints permitting, Jim Hawkins could be found every weekend — Saturdays while his wife, daughter, and grandson did the shopping, and Sundays while his wife, daughter, and grandson did their churching — sitting in that rocker right outside the Manix Store in Augusta, whittling and spitting, spitting and whittling. "Holding court," Big Clem Ellis often called it, but for a king, Jim Hawkins didn't say much.

To the children playing in the streets or on the boardwalk, and even to some younger men, Jim Hawkins sure looked old enough to have been a king, one from those ancient times of Arthur, Richard, George, or Louis. Few knew what age Jim Hawkins might own up to, but Big Clem Ellis said he'd heard that Jim Hawkins was right at fifty years old, which might explain why his hair was so gray, face so sun-beaten underneath that battered gray hat, knuckles so misshapen, or why he needed a scarred hickory cane to push himself out of that rocking chair, especially when it got cold, and it got bitter cold in Augusta. Especially the past winter. Folks figured the Chinooks would never get there, and the warm winds didn't arrive in time for many farmers. Come spring, homesteaders by the score gave up, saying good bye to their mortgages, the unforgiving wind, and forlorn dreams. Bankers would be getting many farms, providing their banks hadn't died, too.

So, there sat Jim Hawkins in front of the Manix Store, rocking and spitting, spitting and whittling, paying little attention to mules pulling buckboards through the mud and muck of Main Street one Saturday afternoon in April. He sent a splash of tobacco juice into a rusty coffee can resting to his right, and never once missed, while other men gathered about as their wives shopped and their children played.

"Good to see you, Jim," Harry Carter said as he settled onto the wooden banister a few feet from where Henry Lancaster, Jim's eleven-year-old grandson, shot marbles with Big Clem Ellis and Hans Junger. "How'd you-all make out this winter?"

"Passable." Jim Hawkins spit.

"Hit forty below in December," Bob Kirk said, "at my place. Coldest I've ever seen it."

"Oh, winter wouldn't have been too bad,"

10

Lou Cator said with a chuckle, "if it hadn't been for the weather."

Everyone laughed at that, except Jim Hawkins, and some pale woman who happened to be riding past the mercantile with her husband in a beat-up old wagon. The wagon bed hauled a sixty-pound moldboard plow, a trunk, and a small coffin. The woman just stared, her eyes as dead as the rest of her face, and she shivered, like she'd never get warm again, and pulled a blanket over her shoulders, not blinking, not really understanding, then turning away. Nobody noticed her except Jim Hawkins and his grandson. All Jim Hawkins did was run his thumb along the edge of his knife for about a minute, then went to work on the stick. Nagged by Big Clem Ellis, young Henry Lancaster stopped staring, and went back to marbles.

"It's the government's fault," Bob Kirk said.

"Usually is," said Pork Ellis, Big Clem's father.

"You blame the government for it being forty below?" Lou Cator asked lightly.

"No," Bob Kirk snapped. "For all this misery. For getting us in that war. Bringing all them fool sodbusters to Montana, telling them to grow wheat, grow wheat, grow wheat. Grow it for the Army, for those starving folks in Europe. Setting the price so it wouldn't drop below two dollars a bushel. Them greedy farmers ruined a lot of good land hereabouts. They're worser than sheepmen."

"Watch it," said Pork Ellis. "I am a sheepman."

"You know what I mean, Pork," Bob went on. "Stock growers like us, we wouldn't ever ruin a land like farmers. But I don't begrudge them none. It's the government."

"First come the war, then the influenza," said J.R. Junger, his accent thick. "Then the winter. Now this misery. It is the end of the world."

"Worst winter that ever struck," Pork Ellis agreed, "iffen you ask me."

"Hard winter," Harry Carter said, "and more hard times coming."

Camdan Gow rode up on a red Indian Big Twin with the white wheels — well, once, maybe, they had been white. For the past two or three years, he had been sputtering around on that motorcycle, which he had special ordered from Massachusetts. Briefly the children abandoned the marbles to study, enviously, Gow's fancy bike, the only motorized vehicle anyone had seen between Helena and Great Falls. Gow, who owned a small ranch just north of Choteau, didn't climb down yet, listening to the conversation and nodding a polite greeting in Jim Hawkins's direction.

"I feel sorry for some of them sodbusters,"

said Lou Cator, no longer smiling.

"I feel sorry for me," Pork Ellis said. "I lost thirty percent of my flock."

"Maybe Governor Stewart can help," Harry Carter offered.

"Well, I ain't buying some bond to build roads," Bob Kirk said, "not to provide relief to a bunch of poor, ignorant . . . what was it they used to call those Texas cattlemen who drove up here?" He was looking to Jim Hawkins for help, but it was Camdan Gow who answered.

"Steer men." Gow stepped off his motorcycle. "And the old-timers were called she-stockmen."

"That ain't what I was thinking," Bob Kirk said.

"Yeah," quipped Lou Cator, "but we got children present."

"Well," Bob Kirk said, "if that bond's the best thing to come out of Helena. . . ." He shook his head, letting the words die.

"Nobody can help them," Gow said as he made his way to the boardwalk.

"What brings you south, Camdan?" Pork Ellis asked.

"Wanted to see how bad things are," the Scotsman answered.

"What's your verdict?" Harry Carter asked him.

Shaking his head, Gow fished a pipe from

the pocket of his jacket.

"Worst winter I can recall," Lou Cator said again.

"Me, too," agreed Harry Carter.

"How about you, Jim?" Pork Ellis asked. "You ever seen a winter that bad?"

The rocking stopped, and Jim Hawkins tossed his slim stick into the mud, folded his knife, and found the handle of the hickory cane. The court stared at him, waiting, and he pulled himself to his feet, and looked through the open doors of the Manix Store. As if summoned, Hawkins's wife and daughter filed out.

"Just one," Jim Hawkins answered at last. "Eighteen Eighty-Six, 'Eighty-Seven." Taking a brown-wrapped package from Mrs. Hawkins, he followed his family down the steps, into the mud, and to his spring wagon.

Harry Carter whistled. "You was here for that one, Jim? That was before my time."

"That was before Augusta," Lou Cator said, laughing.

"Come along, Henry," Jim Hawkins's wife ordered, so the boy quickly put marbles in the pocket of his overalls, and joined the family.

"I have heard the stories," J.R. Junger said.

"Stories that make my bones ache." Harry Carter shook his head.

"Oh," Bob Kirk said, "it couldn't have been as bad as this one. It was snowing at my place *on the Eighth of October."*

"I dunno," Pork Ellis said.

Only Camdan Gow had left the boardwalk, helping the women with their groceries and into the spring wagon before Jim Hawkins snapped the reins, and rubbed his knee as the wagon moved down Main Street.

"How bad was that winter, Jim?" Bob Kirk called out.

"Hard," he answered.

"Worse than this past winter?"

"Harder." He spit into the mud, and flicked the reins eagerly, turning the wagon around in the wide street, heading west, taking his family back toward the Sun River. He stared ahead, eyes pained, remembering something that rose from his soul, thoughts he had tried to forget over the years, memories that strengthened with the stiffness of joints, the whiteness of the hardest of winters, and the bitterest of winds.

Bob Kirk took off his hat to scratch his head. "Well, I don't believe it could have been that bad. Forty below it was, at my place. And that was in early December. Couldn't have been worse than this winter."

"Could have been." Camdan Gow settled into the warm rocker. "And was."

Lou Cator grinned. "Old Jim Hawkins don't say much."

"He said enough," Camdan Gow said.

He said enough.
Jim Hawkins said hardly anything. Ever. That's how Henry Lancaster felt. Sure, he'd hear his grandfather talking to his grandmother fairly often — seemed to be carrying on quite the conversation every now and then — but Jim Hawkins hardly said anything to anybody else.

It was like that on Sunday morning when Henry Lancaster came inside after doing his chores and washing up, finding his mother and grandmother in their Sunday best at the table with Jim Hawkins, who sat quietly making sandwiches of biscuits and bacon for the rest of the day. This Sunday, he was making more sandwiches than usual. Like he had a bunkhouse full of cowhands to feed.

"Eat up," Henry's mother said. "Else we'll be late for preaching."

"Leave the boy with me."

Hearing his grandfather's words, Henry almost choked on crisp bacon.

"It's Sunday," Prudence Lancaster reminded her father.

"Need to do some riding." He started sticking biscuit and bacon sandwiches in the pockets of his Mackinaw.

"It's the Lord's day," Lainie Hawkins said.

16

"He needs to be in church."

"I ain't going to turn Henry into no infidel," Jim Hawkins said. *"Just ride up to the cañon, see things."*

"The cañon!" Prudence shouted. "That'll take you two, three days. Henry'll miss school."

"He can miss a day or two, same as he can miss one sermon. Ain't like the boy hears nothing that preacher says anyway. He's asleep most the time."

Henry's face flushed. So did his grandmother's.

"How would you know, Jim Hawkins?" Lainie snapped.

"You don't need to be riding a horse," Prudence said. "Not that far."

"One reason I need the boy to tag along with me."

"There's nothing up there," Prudence said. "There's no cattle . . . not of yours, anyhow."

"There's memories."

Prudence Lancaster let out a sigh of exasperation, and she was about to argue further, but her mother's face changed, and she was standing, telling Henry to make sure he fetched his bedroll and coat, that it would get cold at night, and then daughter and mother were going at it, but that was a fight Prudence could never win, and the next thing Henry knew, the spring wagon was heading back

17

down the road to Augusta, and he was alone with his grandfather, wondering what was up at Sun River Cañon, and why he wanted an eleven-year-old boy to ride along with him.

"It'll green up," Jim Hawkins said.

"Sir?" the boy asked.

The old cowboy had dismounted the clay-bank gelding, squatting on one of the myriad hills.

Joints creaking, Jim Hawkins stood and swung back into the saddle. "Green up," he repeated. "Usually does after a hard winter. Grass'll grow high, and your mama'll see wildflowers she can't remember ever seeing. It'll be pretty country." He kicked the gelding into a walk. The boy followed along on a small brown mare, moving northwest, toward the circling turkey buzzards they had seen for the past hour.

They came to the fence first, rusted strands of Knickerbocker wire with three-point barbs, running over the hills as far as either Henry Lancaster or Jim Hawkins could see. They rode past the wire trap, stopping when they crested another hill, and stared below at the dead filly, or what was left of her.

She had gotten her left forehoof tangled in the bottom wire, had fallen, struggling to get free, but her efforts had only tightened the wire, cutting to the bone. By the time the wolves came, she hadn't been able to put up much of a fight.

"Stay here." Jim Hawkins handed his grandson the reins, and slowly walked to the remains of the dead horse. He squatted again, touching neither horse nor wire, just staring, then standing, looking ahead, finally letting out a bitter oath, and kicking the fence post, which bent in the muddy soil.

A minute later, he was back in the saddle.

"Should we . . . ?" Henry began.

"Nothing to do," he said, and they rode in silence, until Jim Hawkins started doing something he seldom did. He talked.

CHAPTER TWO

They ride over the hills, which rise like brown waves in an endless sea, toward the rugged Sawtooth range, and Jim Hawkins blurts out: "Ever tell you how I come to Montana?"

"No, sir," the boy replies. He has always figured his grandfather has lived in Montana since the time of dinosaurs.

"Run off from home when I was twelve. Vigo County. In Indiana. Don't remember much about it, the farm, I mean. I remember my ma, my pa, my army of sisters and brothers. Remember them real well. I was the youngest. Pa told me must've been five hundred times that I'd never amount to a farmer. He was right. I knew it then. Didn't want to be no sodbuster. Didn't want nothing to do with Indiana. Wanted to be a cowboy. So I run off, and I don't reckon Pa hunted for me, though it likely worried my ma some. Sold soap. The deal was you sell enough soap, the man I was working for give you a coupon. Get enough

coupons, you trade them in for whatever you desired. So I sold enough soap to clean up half of Fort Smith, Arkansas, which is where I was at that time, then traded in those coupons for a saddle. After that, I drifted down through the Nations and into Texas to learn how to be a cowboy. That's where I met Tommy O'Hallahan. And that's where we both met John Henry Kenton."

"Who were they?" Henry asks.

"They was my pards. Tommy wasn't much older than me. John Henry, he was a good deal older. Took us under his wing. Taught us all a waddie needed to know, or all John Henry thought a waddie needed to know. Reckon we might have stayed in Texas. . . ."

The monologue ceases. The wind blows. The horses crest a hill, and begin riding down, following the fence line.

"Why'd you-all leave?" the boy asks. He expects it's a waste of breath, that his grandfather has returned inside that wall of reticence.

Jim Hawkins doesn't speak for a long while, and Henry Lancaster sighs. The horses' hoofs clop, and they climb the next small hill.

"Wire." Jim Hawkins says at last, his eyes hardening. Another minute passes, another hill, then three more. The boy waits, and, after a soft, whispered curse, the old man is talking *again, pointing at the fence they continue to follow.*

Spring, 1886
Intelligence from the cattle regions of the state are of the gloomiest and most depressing character. The loss in cattle will be great.
— *Chicago Daily Drovers Journal,*
January 13, 1886

CHAPTER THREE

Barbed wire fences. Not like that one, to enclose a pasture. The wire, I mean, was used for what Texicans called a drift fence. Not the same as what some folks up here label a drift fence, big old wooden monsters to handle the snow and mess up a good view of prime country. In the Panhandle of Texas, back in the 'Eighties, it was wire running forever to catch cattle. Well, it caught them, sure enough. That's what we was working on that spring. That's what I picture, what I ain't never been able to get shut of in my mind. All that barbed wire. All them dead cattle.

Ain't so bad, I remember trying to tell myself. *If I can hold my breath, don't think about. . . .*

No luck. Dropping the knife from my right hand, I turned quickly from the drift fence, tried to stumble to the chinaberry tree, but slipped in the mud long before I even neared it. Jerked down the calico bandanna covering my nose and mouth, and vomited, battered hat toppling off my head.

Behind me, come laughter. Tommy O'Hallahan's laughter.

Well, I tried to summon some anger for Tommy, but couldn't. Hell, I'd been laughing at Tommy O'Hallahan that morning when Tommy mixed his breakfast with Panhandle mud.

Serves me right, I figured, not that I'd ever tell Tommy so. I just let him laugh, till I reckon he had to stop before he started to throw up again. The smell was that bad, but it wasn't just the smell, it was the flies. Thousands of them. And maggots. Mostly, I reckon, it was all that waste. Or maybe it was what we was doing. Skinning dead cattle. More than you could count.

I was breathing heavily, waiting to see if the nausea had passed. Hoped so. Didn't have nothing left in my belly to lose.

The way I recollect, I hadn't thrown up since that September, back when John Henry Kenton had passed out at The Equity Bar in Tascosa, leaving behind three-quarters of a bottle of Chicken Cock & Rye. At least, that's what the label on the bottle said, or so Tommy had told me. Us two kids had dragged our pard to McCormick's livery, then sampled the whiskey ourselves. Next thing I knew, I was dreaming that I was vomiting up my supper in my sougans. Only when I woke up, I realized it hadn't been no dream. Couldn't hold down a meal for two more days, but I had learned a mighty important lesson. Swore I'd never touch another bottle of Chicken Cock & Rye. Tommy, of course, hadn't made no such a promise, but Tommy hadn't been airing his paunch that time. And John Henry? Boy howdy, how he laughed, till he realized he had paid for that rye and hadn't gotten to enjoy much of it himself, forgetting that he had killed one bottle already. John Henry was fifteen, maybe twenty years older than us. Maybe even older. Wouldn't swear that he was any smarter, though. Smarter than me, I suppose, but not Tommy. No, sir. Tommy was smart enough to be a schoolmaster. He'd read more books than I'd ever seen, which is why the boys at the 7K called him Professor when we was riding for that brand.

That reminds me. The hands at the 7K had dubbed me Rye the rest of the season, and eventually I had learned to laugh with them. Having Rye for a handle sure beat Suds, which was what the older cowboys had called me on the first outfit I had worked for, and Soapy, which is what John Henry Kenton took to calling me when we'd first started riding together. On account of my saddle bought with soap coupons.

Good times, back then. Before that spring.

Things was different after '86. This was work. Sickening, gruesome work. Me and Tommy wasn't the only boys who couldn't hold down his breakfast. Older hands also gagged, vomited. Bitter as bile what we was doing.

Still dizzy, I managed to pick up my hat, set it back on my head, and slowly rose, wiping my forehead with a mud-caked right hand, cleaning up my mouth and chin with that raggedy old bandanna, which I then pulled back over my nose and mouth. I moved back to the barbed wire fence, and the dead cattle. I was drawing time, and always figured a good cowhand put in a good day's work for a good day's wages. Not that $1 a day and found was what anybody in his right mind would consider good wages. But we was cowboys on the open range. That's all that mattered.

"Feel better?" Tommy asked once I had fetched the knife and went back to work skinning the bloated carcass of a long-dead steer whose brand no one recognized.

For two days we'd been at it, Tommy, me, and John Henry Kenton, and just about every other cowboy from Tascosa to Mobeetie, south nigh down to Memphis, and west thirty-five miles past the New Mexico Territory line. Riders from the T Anchor and the Turkey Track, the LE, LIT, Ladder 3E, 7K, Box T, even Mr. Charles Goodnight's JA.

"Devil's rope," John Henry said a few rods down the fence, working on another long-horn, his leather gloves soaked with blood and mud. That's what we called the wire. That's what it was. That's how I saw it back then. Ofttimes, I still do. "Ought to use it to hang every. . . ." John Henry lifted his bandanna to spit, then shook his head, and went back to work.

Well, I looked up at Tommy, who swallowed, 'cause we hadn't forgotten. We'd helped put up part of that drift fence the summer before, using barbed wire. And John Henry Kenton had dug his share of post holes, and stretched miles upon miles of those two-twisted strands with the H-shaped barb patented by Mr. Hiram B. Scutt. I ain't never forgotten that wire. Don't see how I could, as much of it as I saw down in Texas. Yeah, John Henry had done his share of sweating and cursing alongside us boys stringing that devil's rope.

I'd best backtrack some, let you know how things got to be the way they was in Texas in the spring of '86. Let you know how we come to be skinning dead cattle.

The 7K had let us three go in November. Not enough work in the winter, so we'd been riding the grubline through Christmas, before Mickey McCormick had hired Tommy to work at the livery till spring, and John Henry had talked Booger Pete into letting me swamp the saloon for the winter — me and Tommy later come to the conclusion that John Henry wanted to have friends in the right places, where he could get a few drinks and board his horse, or sleep off a drunk. John Henry, of course, would do no job he couldn't do from a saddle, most times anyway, or so he said, so he spent the winter wandering from ranch to ranch, working for a meal. Me and Tommy wished we had been riding with him.

At first.

Things changed on Wednesday night, January 6th. Some dates a man just never forgets, like his birthday, wedding day, things like that. Of course, I remember the morning your ma was born. Well, January 6, 1886, was one of those dates. Won't never forget that one, either.

Wasn't supposed to get that cold in Texas, you see, and it never snowed that much. Even the winter of '84–85 wasn't this bad, and John Henry Kenton said it was as hard as they came. A soldier boy from Fort Elliott had staggered into Booger Pete's when I was fixing coffee, saying the wind was roaring right under sixty miles an hour. Folks even said ice formed on Galveston Bay, although I ain't rightly sure I believed that story. Texicans could tell some falsehoods. Yet it had been plenty cold, ten below zero at Mobeetie.

Down in Tascosa, Tommy O'Hallahan later told me, the snow turned black. Black snow! I ain't doubting it, not for a minute. The brutal wind picked up sand, mixing with snow, dark, ugly, stinging anyone who stepped outside. That's what Tommy told me, and he wouldn't lie to me, not back then. Mickey McCormick's livery wasn't the most comfortable place to wait out a blizzard, either, but Tommy, like me, had a roof over his head. We wasn't sure about John Henry.

I worried about our pard. Our mentor, really. Reckon Tommy did his share of worrying, too. John Henry was a forty-year-old cowhand, without a job, riding from bunkhouse to bunkhouse across the Panhandle, waiting for spring. A man caught out in this storm could die. I knew that plain enough even before Mr. Les Carter hauled them five corpses to town in the back of a wagon.

Mr. Carter, a stove-up old belly-cheater who'd been let go and was also riding the grubline, said he found a covered wagon over along the Canadian River, a team of sorrels frozen in the harness, and inside a man, woman, and three children, dead. Somehow, Mr. Carter got the dead horses out of the frozen harness, hitched his buckskin gelding to the wagon, and brought the dead family to Mobeetie.

Town undertaker had to wait till the ground was soft enough to bury that unlucky family. You know, I thought about those poor folks yesterday when we was in Augusta, and them poor sodbusters come to town in that wagon, with that little coffin in the back. Maybe that's why I'm telling you all this. Maybe it's because I just ain't never told nobody, not even your grandmother, about all that happened, although Lainie knows a bunch of it, seen a bunch of it herself. Maybe it's because I wasn't that much older than you. Maybe it's because it's something I've been needing to get off my chest for better than thirty years.

When the storm finally broke, I'd never

seen so much snow, not even when I was a younker in Indiana. Three or four feet on the streets, and drifts climbed even higher. The roof on Luke Potter's adobe house had collapsed under the weight. It took a month before the stagecoach from New Mexico Territory started running again.

A bad winter.

Spring was worse.

John Henry rode into Mobeetie in February, with Tommy trotting along right behind him on a claybank. They stopped at Booger Pete's for John Henry's morning bracer and to pick me up. Winter might have been hard, but spring came early to Texas, and there was work to do.

"Got us a job at the Ladder 3E," John Henry announced.

Me? I was more interested in the winter. "How'd you make out in that blizzard?"

"Colder than a witch's caress." John Henry killed the shot of whiskey, and refilled his glass.

"Thought you might have froze to death," I said, still picturing those poor folks Mr. Carter had found.

"Me, too," Tommy added.

John Henry had lifted the glass to his lips, but slowly lowered it, smiling. "You boys are still mighty green. A little snow ain't gonna kill John Henry Kenton." The shot glass raised again to be slammed on the cherry-wood bar, empty. "Let's ride. Spring gather will commence soon."

Only, long before we reached the Ladder 3E headquarters, we was wondering if there would be any cattle to round up.

We found the remains in bogs, at the bottom of bluffs, in the Canadian River, but mostly piled up against the drift fence. The air had turned rancid, filled with flies and the stench of rot.

Twice, we come to arroyos — that's what they called them down in Texas; we call them coulées up this way — that was filled with so many dead cattle that a man could ride across and not even touch the dirt. If his horse would let him, though no horse would. Things was that bad.

Dead cattle was everywhere.

At a tent revival meeting in Clarendon, some sky pilot preached that this was all God's will, and His sheep had to accept His wishes, but neither me nor Tommy could see why the Almighty would want to kill tens of thousands of poor dumb cows. Nor did John Henry, and he told that preacher man a thing or two. Well, Clarendon had never been real popular with cowboys, and us cowboys had never been popular with anybody who lived in that town. Some old Methodist had founded it as what they called a "sobriety settlement" that didn't cater or cotton to cowhands. "Saints Roost" is what most of us cowboys called the place. Only reason we'd stopped there was to buy coffee and tobacco. You couldn't get a drink of whiskey there.

"Wasn't God's doing!" Kenton yelled at that Methodist. "It was our own!"

He was right, I reckon. Partly anyhow. It was the wire. The wire we'd help string up.

"Cattle ain't like all critters," John Henry had told me and Tommy more times than either of us could remember. "They drift. Just turn their hindquarters to the wind and start walking."

During the winter of 1881–82, back when I was still just a-wasting away on that farm in Indiana, cattle had drifted onto the Texas ranges down from the Arkansas River. Even as far as the Platte. Come spring, the beef that hadn't died in the winter was chewing up Panhandle grass.

I don't have to tell you how much value a stock grower puts on grass. Can't afford to have a bunch of cattle from some place else eating grass growed for his beef. They was picking Texas grass clean. Now, all this here information is second-hand. Like I say, I was just a poor, dumb farm boy around then, but the story I'm relating here is true. John Henry told us about it. He wasn't one to lie to me or Tommy, either. Not then.

So cowboy crews had to come to Texas from Nebraska, Colorado, even a few from Wyoming, to gather up their cattle. And it wasn't like the Texas cows hadn't drifted. That year, John Henry was a floater, looking for strays for the brand he was riding for, and he spent much of that spring wandering down along the Blanco River. A right far piece from his range.

Anyhow, when everything got sorted out, when the Wyoming cowhands took their beeves back to Wyoming, and so forth, when John Henry had come back to the Panhandle, a good deal of winter grass was ruined. That's when the ranchers started putting up wire because the Panhandle Stock Raisers Association had met in Mobeetie and come to the conclusion to build a drift fence.

They got the posts from the Canadian River breaks, or the Palo Duro. Cost them big ranchers $200 a mile, even more, to string that fence. But they kept putting up wire.

Remember that time we all had to ride down to Helena, and your ma asked me to take you to see that 10¢ moving-picture show? The one with that fellow dressed up like a cowboy, only I don't think he knew which end of a horse was what? You remember that? Figured you did. You seemed to like it. Remember that cowboy's boss, the big rancher, and how he wanted to run off all those sodbusters because they was putting up barbed wire fences? He started preaching about the open range, and farmers was ruining the West. Well, it wasn't always like that, boy. Yeah, farmers put up fences, but so did a bunch of cattlemen. And they done it for the same reason.

To keep the cattle out.

By the time I'd come down to Texas, and after I'd met up with Tommy, and then John Henry had took us on and started looking after us green peas, well, there was a lot of barbed wire running across the Panhandle. We kept putting up wire.

I'd best explain one thing. It wasn't just one long fence. No. Ranchers ain't got the temperament to work like that, work together like that, I mean, so all those fences didn't connect. Probably about the year I started cowboying, there was a law made that said you had to put in gates, and gateways had to be so wide and so forth. So this drift fence was really a series of long fences, and a cowboy on a good cow pony could find a way through that . . . guess you'd call it a maze. If it was a right sunny day. If the cowboy wasn't too stupid. But the thing is this . . . cows are stupid. They couldn't find a way through those fences. Come a hard winter, a bad blizzard, cows would just drift till they come to a fence, or a river, or a coulée, and they'd just stop. They'd just stop and stand there, till they died.

That's what had happened with that terrible blizzard. That's why me and Tommy and John Henry had lowered ourselves to skin dead cattle that spring.

Maybe we would have stayed in Texas, kept right on skinning carcasses, but I reckon John Henry would have blowed his top before long, and up and quit. Which is pretty much what he did, what we all did, but it didn't happen till I stepped on that cactus.

CHAPTER FOUR

I was wearing boots. Good boots, too, not like them Congress gaiters your ma thinks you need to wear to church and school. Lord, your ma never has quite come to grips with the fact that we live on a small ranch in the middle of nowhere. Sometimes, I find it hard to believe that a girl like that was raised by your grandma and me. Good woman, now, don't get me wrong, but she sure ain't a ranch woman. Your pa, before he had to run off and join Pershing's Doughboys and get himself killed, rest in peace, liked his boots, too. He's probably turning over in his grave seeing you in those confounded shoes.

Anyway, I was talking about my boots. Tall boots they was, the color of midnight, with blue crescent moons inlaid in the tops. Just like the ones John Henry wore, only he had stars instead of moons, and his stars was white. I'd spent $13 on them in Tascosa, and I had on a pair of thick wool socks. And the cactus was just a little old prickly pear that was growing alongside the drift fence, and I had finished skinning one dead steer and was moving to work on another, and just slipped.

The only way I can figure it is that my right foot slid right into that prickly pear at just the right place, so those long old spines poked through that boot right where the foot meets the outsole. Had I stepped on the cactus, had I slid into that prickly pear any other way, nothing would have happened other than I would have cursed, Tommy would have laughed and called me clumsy, and I would have started cutting up the dead steer, waving away the flies, trying to keep the disgust from rising in my throat, probably thinking how that farm in Vigo County, Indiana wouldn't look so bad along about now.

Didn't happen that way, though.

The cactus spines stabbed me good and hard, and I let out a howl. Screamed like somebody had chopped off my right foot, which is about how it felt. Maybe it was on account of how tired I was.

John Henry and Tommy, they was good pards. They was running to me through all that mud, leaping over the rotting remains of cattle, coming to my rescue.

Well, I got the boot pulled off, seemed surprised to see my foot intact, but, thunderation, those cactus spines hurt. Tommy, he saw that I wasn't hurt bad, and he had to start sniggering, saying that it wasn't like I'd been bit by a rattlesnake, and how he wished I'd put my sock and boot back on because they stank worser than the dead cattle.

"It ain't funny!" I snapped right back at him. Pouting I was. Well, I was only fifteen years old. Just a fool kid, though I thought of myself as a man, just the way Tommy did.

"How'd you do that?" Tommy asked. "I mean, get them spears through your boots?"

"I don't know." I rubbed the side of my foot, then, still mad, pride hurting now more than my foot, pulled on my sock and boot. "You wouldn't think it was so funny if you. . . ."

Tommy headed me off. "I wouldn't fall into a prickly pear."

I was on my feet now, feeling that blood rush to my head, knowing my ears must have been redder than a rose, and I suspect me and Tommy would have started trading blows. We'd do that from time to time, boys being boys, cowboys being cowboys. We could fight something awful. I'd bloody his nose, he'd bust my lip, and we'd later realize we had been trading punches over nothing. But if some worthless saddle tramp was to insult me, or start fighting me, well, Tommy would be the first one to join the fracas. I'd do the same for him. Had done the same, by grab, like that time at Doan's Store.

That was Tommy. A man to ride the river with.

John Henry Kenton, he felt the same. That time at Doan's that I just mentioned, when a couple of old peckerwoods had grabbed Tommy from behind and started punching him over something Tommy had said, well, I'd jumped in to help my pard, but them two peckerwoods were mighty strong, and I wasn't having much effect on the outcome of that fight. But John Henry Kenton, he came out of the store, lariat in his hand, and he lit into those old boys and beat them senseless with that rope, whipping them, cutting their faces to their cheek bones. Beat them something ugly, and might could have killed them. It took two strong men to pull John Henry off those peckerwoods. Awful temper John Henry had. You never wanted to get him riled, but you sure wanted him on your side.

The three of us was like the Musketeers,

Tommy told me once. That's a book Tommy had once read.

I'm rattling on as senseless as one of those old reprobates at the Manix Store, ain't I? Where was I? Oh, yeah, the fight me and Tommy was fixing to have along the drift fence.

John Henry stopped it.

Only, he wasn't paying much attention to me and Tommy. What he did was just kick the tarnation out of the nearest fence post, kicked it so hard it started leaning to the east in that drying mud, and with that, me and Tommy was staring at him, and John Henry was just looking down that long line of wire, his gloved hands clenched so tight his whole body was shaking.

We stood silent, a little worried.

"This ain't right."

I wasn't sure I'd heard John Henry right, he'd spoken so soft, and usually you never had to ask John Henry Kenton what he had just said. I wasn't about to ask him to repeat himself, though, and he let out this long sigh, then pulled off those gloves he was wearing and tossed them on the dead steer.

"No, sir," he said, louder now. "It ain't right." He swore, and turned to me and Tommy, mud and grime and blood caked on his beard stubble, brown eyes almost as black now as his boots.

"Ain't right. Ain't suitable. Ain't befitting us. I don't know what we were thinking. Tommy, you ought to have known better." He looked at me. "You lame?"

"No, sir," I said right back to him, and I was picking up my knife, thinking John Henry was pestering me to get back to work, but Tommy, he was smart, and he stopped me from making a bigger fool out of myself. He just reached out and grabbed my arm, pulled me back, and gave this slight gesture with his jaw to pay attention to John Henry Kenton.

Which is what both of us done.

"You think this is a job for a cowhand?" John Henry asked, but he wasn't really talking to us boys, he was talking to himself. Practicing, I think, for what he'd tell Jenks Foster, who did the hiring and the firing at the Ladder 3E.

"I ain't drawing time for something I can't do on the back of a horse," he said. "Men pay me to nurse cattle, not skin them. I must have gone plumb out of my head to hire on for a job like this. Let's go."

We saddled our horses, and rode away from the drift fence. John Henry left his gloves where he had dropped them. No matter. They was ruined from all that blood and guts.

I don't think we said a word on the whole long ride back to the Ladder 3E headquarters. Jenks Foster was sitting on his rocking chair on the porch of the bunkhouse when we rode up late that afternoon, like he was expecting us.

A good man, Jenks Foster. He had a chaw of tobacco inside his mouth that stretched his cheek out like he was eating a whole apple, and sat in that rocking chair, working his tobacco, and braiding something with horsehair. He wore a big hat, shapeless, covered with dirt from years on the ranges, plaid pants stuck in stovepipe boots, plaid shirt, and calico bandanna. And spurs with the biggest set of rowels that I'd ever seen.

I liked old Jenks Foster. At the Ladder 3E, folks said Jenks had gone on drives to Abilene back when it was wild and cantankerous. They said he had worked with men like Shanghai Pierce and Ike Pryor. They said he had ridden on that first drive on what we later called the Goodnight-Loving Trail. He was a cowman all the way through, and I hated to quit him like we was about to do.

He spit onto the ground, and set aside his horsehair, and just rocked, waiting, like he was expecting us to come.

"If I wanted to be a skinner," John Henry told him without getting down from his horse, "I'd have hired on with some buffalo-running outfit."

"No buffalo outfits anymore, Kenton," Jenks Foster said easily. "Not in a long, long time. No buffalo, either."

"I draw time as a cowpuncher," John Henry said. "I work on the back of a horse. Skinning rotting cattle ain't a job for me."

Foster's bronzed head nodded. "Don't blame you. You'll be drawing your time, I reckon."

"Figure I got two weeks coming."

"And you?" Now, Jenks Foster was looking right at me.

"We's pards." It was all I could think of to say.

Old Jenks, he smiled at that, which made me feel a whole lot better, especially when he looked away from me and at Tommy. "You feel the same, Tommy?"

"Yes, sir."

"You want your books?" Jenks asked. "Along with the pay you got coming?"

"The books?" Tommy blinked. "Those books are yours, Jenks."

"Not mine. They come with the bunkhouse. Don't know who first brought them to the Ladder 3E, but the only time they ever got read was by you. Pack them in your war bag, Tommy."

Jenks stood, spit again. "I'll get what money I owe you."

One of the books was by Balzac. I don't remember the title, but I do recall that Jenks Foster said he'd sure miss "that potbellied son-of-a-gun" and how Tommy used to read after supper. We'd packed up our possibles, which didn't amount to much, other than the three books Tommy was getting as a bonus. I'd hoped to eat supper at the ranch, but the place was deserted that evening. It was going to be a long walk to Tascosa.

Should point out that we didn't own our horses, just our saddles and tack. The Ladder 3E had a company rule that cowboys couldn't own their own mounts. Bunch of ranches done things the same way. So we'd laid out our war bags with our saddles and bridles on the porch, got our envelopes from Jenks Foster — didn't bother opening them up to count the cash because we trusted Jenks. And we just stood there, waiting, knots on a log.

"Where's Fussy?" John Henry asked. Fussy was the cook. His name was Fussell, but everyone called him Fussy. Big fat guy, chewed on long-nine cigars all the time till they was soggy and torn up. Never smoked them. Just chewed on them.

"Let him go," Jenks Foster said.

"Let him go?" John Henry turned, facing our ex-boss like he was about to go for his six-shooter. My mouth dropped open, too. Fussy wasn't much of a cook, and I got tired of finding shreds of cigars in my beans, but he was a good man, quick with a joke, and I'd worked for worse belly-cheaters.

After spitting out a mouthful of tobacco juice, Jenks Foster said: "You count how many cattle you skinned?"

"No," John Henry fired back.

"I have. You and all the other outfits I had out there. The way things have averaged out, it comes to one hundred and seventy-nine per mile. Over twenty-six miles." He looked over at Tommy. "Son, you're mighty good with words. How are you at ciphering? Can you figure that out?"

"Well. . . ." Tommy sort of grinned. Oh, he could figure out a problem like that, but he'd need a pencil and paper, and some time.

"Four thousand, six hundred, fifty-four," Jenks Foster said. "That's just along the drift fence." He was looking back at John Henry. "John Hollicot come over yesterday

47

from the LX. He's lost twice as many."

"Wire." John Henry's fists were clenched tight again. He cursed the wire.

"It's bad. Bad as I've ever seen. So I let Fussy go. Nobody to cook for here, anyhow, except me." He let out a list of names of other riders for the Ladder 3E who had come in and quit. I think that disappointed John Henry. He'd hoped he had been the first one to show his pride, but, turns out, we was among the last.

"Clu Marshall, Lavender Mills, and Chet Muller are still out there," Jenks Foster said. "Lavender ain't got the sense God gave a horned toad. He'll skin cattle all the way to Kansas if he ain't careful. They are the only ones left riding for the Ladder 3E."

"You'll fire them, too?" John Henry asked.

"Didn't fire you, did I? You boys quit. Like the rest of them, except Fussy, and he'll find a job somewhere else, or give up this crazy way of life, go to work in some restaurant. No, the Ladder 3E ain't finished. Lavendar'll stay on. Same as Chet. Clu? Probably not. Not when he finds out that he'll have to eat my cooking till things recover down here. There's work to be done. Hides to be picked up. Watering holes to be cleaned. Wire to be fixed. You boys could stay on, if you had a mind."

"I reckon not," John Henry said. "We'll drift."

Me and Tommy nodded our agreement.

"Figured as much. Don't blame you. There'll be some tramps and drunks, bottom of the barrel, and greenhorns in the saloons. I'll hire some of those boys to do the jobs needed to be done around here."

Silence filled the night. Coyotes started yipping. Jenks Junior, which is the name we'd saddled on the cur dog on the ranch, started yipping right back till those coyotes stopped making all that noise.

"You boys need me to put in a word for you, I'd be right proud to do so." Jenks spit again. "The only thing is this . . . jobs might be hard to come by in these parts. This year. For work befitting cowhands like you."

"Is it that bad?" Tommy asked.

"Bad enough," Jenks answered. "You saw it yourself. Skinning cattle. I'm thinking forty percent here. I hear the XIT is saying only fifteen percent. And I've heard some bookkeepers say that a bunch of us ranchers are exaggerating our losses, killing off what they call the book count, and not the actual count."

"You bring those bookkeepers to that fence," John Henry said, his voice hoarse, edgy, "and you ask them if that stink comes from paper."

"Know what you mean, Kenton." Jenks moved that mound of tobacco to his other cheek. "Tommy," he said, "if you'd hitch up the spring wagon, I'll give you boys a ride to Tascosa. No need in you boys having to walk all that way, lugging your traps."

Tommy took off. I should have followed him, helped him, but I didn't. I figured Jenks Foster expected me to go, too, wanted to tell John Henry something private, but I wasn't about to go till I'd heard him say something. That's the one mistake I ever saw Jenks Foster make. He should have asked both of us to go hitch that team.

"The Quarter Circle Heart is going out of business," Jenks said. "Lost fifty percent over there. I'm sorry, Kenton. Know you used to ride for that brand. Didn't want you to travel all the way over to Donley County for a job that ain't there."

"Hadn't planned on it," John Henry said.

"Can I ask where you're thinking about going? Might know somebody there who could use three good hands."

"Somewhere," John Henry said, "where there's no wire fences."

CHAPTER FIVE

Turned out to be Montana. At least, that's what we thought, or what John Henry Kenton thought. 'Course, it was a rather round-about way that we got here.

First, John Henry blew all of his pay in Tascosa. Then he blew half of our pay, mine and Tommy's, that he'd asked us to loan him. Only then, after John Henry had sobered up and gotten something in his stomach that was solid and not forty-rod, we started looking for a job. But our luck was on hold. The only job we could get was with dead cattle, only it was a whole lot better than skinning them.

The Texas Cattle Raisers Association sent out instructions to all its members to please send all of the cattle hides to the market in Dodge City, Kansas. That way, the brass figured, the Texas Cattle Raisers Association would have a better idea of just how bad things were after the blizzard. So we got a job as freighters, hauling wagons from around Fort Elliott to Dodge City, tossing our saddles and bridles on top of those stinking hides. Hired on with Captain Andrew J. Jonas, the boss of the train, and he was a boss, let me tell you. He had lost his left arm all the way plumb up to his elbow during the war. Either at Gettysburg or Shiloh, charging with John Bell Hood or swinging a saber with Ulysses S. Grant, depending on who asked him, or how much John Barleycorn he'd poured down his gullet. Of course, Tommy, he suspicioned Captain Jonas's stories, said he didn't believe our boss had even fought in the War Between the States, yet Tommy never said so to the captain's face.

Wasn't hard work as skinning dead cattle, or digging fence posts, or stringing barbed wire, though we had to work with mules, and I told Tommy that he had finally found a job that fitted him to a T. All he had to do was sit on his backside and yell cuss words.

Wasn't easy, though. It was turning hot. Hides attracted a million flies. Mules are stubborn, ignorant critters. Handling a team, freighting double-hitched wagons across the Panhandle and into Indian Territory and through southwestern Kansas was a chore. I'm talking about a team of twelve mules, hitched to two wagons with a little old repair caboose trailing the wagons. Loaded sky-high with stinking hides. That's what each of us had to handle. John Henry worked the wagons right behind Captain Jonas's team, followed by a couple others whose names I forgot years ago, then Tommy, with me riding drag. Tommy and me had drawed straws to see who come out sucking the hind teat, and Tommy's luck generally run better than mine.

Me and Tommy wasn't cut out for that job, but we done our best. Most of those muleskinners avoided us, ignored us, never talked to us, and looked at us with contempt, probably disgust, but there was one fellow who kept us two boys from making bigger fools out of ourselves. Probably kept Captain Jonas from firing us, and firing John Henry because it was John Henry who had spoke up for us, gotten us the jobs. Anyway, this 'skinner, name was Harris, he helped us each morning and evening with the teams, gave us a few tips on what to do, sort of looked after us, which was more than John Henry done on that long, hot, stinking, dusty trip.

I'll tell you true, muleskinning and freighting ain't no jobs befitting a cowboy. John Henry must have done it before, and, like I said, he told a few falsehoods about me and Tommy having some experience before, which is one reason Captain Jonas hired us. Truthfully the main reason we got hired was that four or five of his 'skinners had quit on him in Mobeetie, and pickings was slim for the return trip to Kansas. He filled one job with a soldier who had quit the Army, or the Army had made him quit, and Captain Jonas had to drive the other wagon himself. Usually he just bossed the job, or so he told us. That left him three muleskinners needed, and that's where me and Tommy and John Henry come in. Now, we wasn't the only cowboys out of work, but we was the only three who'd agree to work for his wages and do his kind of work. Most cowboys wouldn't, and mostly on account of pride.

Fact is, I couldn't figure out why John Henry had agreed to such a job, and I up and told him so one night. I was sore, in more ways than one, 'cause I'd just gotten the daylights walloped out of me by a big sorrel jack that had kicked me so hard, I wouldn't be sitting on my backside for the next day or two. Didn't see how I was going to be able to sit on the wheeler and keep those mules moving, no matter how hard I kicked the wheeler's ribs, how loud I cussed, or how hard I cracked that blacksnake whip.

"It'll get us to Dodge City," John Henry answered.

"And then what?" I fired right back.

"Then we get us a real job." John Henry grinned. "I hear the nights turn real cool in Montana."

"Montana?" Tommy sang out. That was the first we'd ever heard about Montana.

"Montana," John Henry said. "Good cow country. Lot of ranchers in Texas and Kansas have been shipping herds north. Boy I met in Fort Worth told me you wouldn't believe the gathers they have in the Judith Basin. Says a man can mount his horse in Miles City and ride all the way to the Bitterroots and not see farmer or fence. That's where we're bound, boys. Montana."

Sounded good to me. As long as it was far from Vigo County, Indiana.

"Montana." Tommy tested the word, his head bobbing. "Well, I hope, for Jim's sake, that there are no prickly pear cactus in Montana. Leave him bawling like a baby sister."

If my rear-end hadn't been so sore from that mule's hoof, Tommy and I would have had another go of fisticuffs.

We made it to Dodge City in one piece, and I ain't never lowered myself to freight noth-

55

ing for nobody since then. Well, hardly since then. Had to haul supplies for ranches, things like that, but that's different. Captain Jonas paid us off, even asked John Henry — but not me or Tommy — if he'd hire on with him again. The captain was going to freight some whiskey to Mobeetie and Tascosa, then come back with another load of hides. There was a lot of hides that year. I recollect hearing Captain Jonas say the man he sold his load to had already bought 32,579. That's how bad that winter had been.

"I'll stick to cowboying," John Henry told him.

"There's no future in cattle," Captain Jonas argued. "Cattle are fetching ten dollars a head, not thirty. Hides are of more value than a steer. You'd do well to reconsider."

John Henry hooked a thumb back at me and Tommy, who was leaning against a hitching post on Front Street, waiting for our pard. "I got them two kiddoes to look after. We'll push north."

That was the first time me or Tommy had ever been to Dodge. Queen of the Cow Towns. That's what she was. I'd been to Fort Smith in Arkansas, and Fort Worth, and The Flat in Texas, and Baxter Springs in Kansas, and, of course, towns like Tascosa and Mobeetie, but none of them could hold a candle to Dodge City. Wanted to be able to take in the sights, see some hootchie-cootchie show, maybe even try to buck the tiger at a faro table, but I hardly got even a look at Dodge. John Henry took us to a bathhouse while he went to get himself a whiskey, and by the time Tommy and me come out all clean, even behind our ears, John Henry had lined up another job for us.

Things wasn't so bad in Kansas. Not in Dodge City, at least. Oh, the market was hurting, like Captain Jonas said, with the price for cattle dropping, and, if I remember right, I think 400,000 was the number of cowhides that was shipped out of Dodge that year. That's just Dodge. Ain't no telling how many hides was just left for the coyotes and turkey vultures. Don't know how many hides was shipped from other places.

But cattle was moving. Drovers wasn't stopping them in Dodge to get shipped out East, not for no $10 a head. They was pointing those herds north, to fatten up on better pastures in Wyoming and Montana, to wait for the market to recover. So we got hired on by an outfit driving 2,200 steers to Ogallala, Nebraska. Me and Tommy rode drag the whole time. Never ate so much dust, but, like I say, it was a whole lot better than what we had been doing that spring in the Texas Panhandle. And from Nebraska, we went even farther north, pushing another herd when we got hired to help take some cattle on into Montana.

Miles City it was. Place was full of Texas cowboys and Texas longhorns — although both cows and cowhands looked half starved — and I figured we'd just hire out there, but that's not what John Henry Kenton had in mind. The boss man of the outfit we had worked for, Bill Bennett, the one that took 2,500 four-year-olds from Ogallala to Miles City, he said he knew this feller who was shipping three breeding bulls to Helena, and this feller was looking for three cowboys to play nursemaid to those bulls, get them to Helena, then push them up to the Sun River range.

We wandered over to the man at the Northern Pacific depot, and he looked us over, talked to John Henry a minute or two, then took us down the tracks to this car, and let all three of us peek inside.

"What the Sam Hill are they?" John Henry asked the fellow.

And the fellow replied: "Aberdeen Angus. Spectacular-looking animals, aren't they?

As black as a raven's wing at midnight. I have papers on all three from the American Aberdeen Angus Association in Chicago." He spoke with a thick Scottish accent, like he'd just stepped off the boat from Aberdeen.

The bulls didn't seem interested in nothing the man had to say. Didn't look so spectacular to me.

"Those three boys can trace their lineage back to Old Jock and Old Granny, Hugh Watson's original Angus doddies." The man passed out cigars to all three of us. "You have experience with cattle?"

"Longhorns," John Henry answered.

"Sturdy animals, your Texas beef," the Scotsman said as he lighted John Henry's cigar. Tommy was still staring at his. I'd put mine in my vest pocket. "You'll find the Aberdeen Angus also strong. With an even temperament, but not as timid as any Hereford. They adapt well to their environs, and their marbled meat is better than any beef I've ever tasted."

"Wouldn't know." John Henry smiled. "Eat your own beef, it'll make you sick."

Well, the Scotsman roared with laughter over that one, and I knew we had the job right then and there. Didn't need no recommendation from Bill Bennett.

"But those bulls don't even have horns," Tommy blurted out.

"No, they don't, laddie, but those black bulls are tough. Only one thing you need to know about Angus." The man grinned. "All cattle will kick. But an Angus never misses." He held out his hand. "The name's Gow. Tristram Gow."

And that's how we come to Montana. Took those bulls with Tristram Gow — Camdan's pa — from Miles City, through Billings, all the way to Helena. Then herded them north to the Sun River range.

Chapter Six

Henry Lancaster and his grandfather have camped on the treeless hills, sitting by the campfire in the midnight blackness and cool of spring, sipping coffee. Jim Hawkins has turned taciturn once more, uttering fewer than a dozen words since that afternoon, and the boy is disappointed. He had longed to hear tales of glory, danger, stampedes, gunfights, and wild Indians on the cattle drives, but Jim Hawkins covered those weeks on the trail with little comment.

Now, both are silent, until the grandfather pulls a pint bottle from his coat pocket, and sweetens his coffee.

"I thought. . . ." The boy gambles on his words, grinning to show his grandfather that he isn't serious. "Thought you told me that you swore off chicken whiskey after you got sick that time."

His grandfather chuckles, corks the bottle, which disappears. He tastes his coffee.

"Chicken Cock and Rye," he corrects. "I did. I've never touched a drop of Chicken Cock and Rye since that autumn in Texas." Another sip. "But this is Dewar's." That's all he says, until he sets down the empty tin cup. "Whiskey's all right, boy, as long as you don't let it best you."

A longer silence.

"You see that?"

Jim Hawkins points at the black, star-filled sky.

"What?" Henry asks. "The stars?"

"The Big Dipper."

A moment passes. "Oh, yeah," Henry says. "There's the Little Dipper, too. Find it, and you find the North Star."

"Looks like it's ladling out some good, cold water from the Sun River."

"Huh?"

After a short chuckle, Jim Hawkins says: "That's what John Henry Kenton told me and Tommy."

Henry has stepped away from the fire, staring harder at the bowl of the Big Dipper, but now he looks curiously at his grandfather. Jim Hawkins retrieves the flask of Dewar's, takes a long pull, and returns the bottle, shaking his head. As Tommy returns to the campfire, his grandfather is talking again.

Summer, 1886

. . . the prospects for stock men are not of a
flattering nature, and it would seem to us
that those who place pilgrim cattle upon
the ranges this year are doing an unwise and
unprofitable business.

— *Bozeman Chronicle,*
July 31, 1886

CHAPTER SEVEN

Me and Tommy were tired — just plain
whipped, I tell you — by the time we got
those Angus bulls to the Dee & Don Rivers
Land and Cattle Company, Incorporated.
The Bar DD brand. Most folks called it the
MacDunn Ranch, but the MacDunns didn't
own it. It was run by board of directors in
Aberdeen, Scotland. No, that ain't right,
either. It was run by Major MacDunn, William
Bruce MacDunn, and that's why folks
between Helena and Great Falls called it
the MacDunn Ranch, or MacDunn Empire,
even if Major MacDunn had to report to
the board of directors across the Atlantic
Ocean.

All that time on the train ride from Miles
City to Helena, us three cowboys keeping
three black bulls company while Mr. Gow
rode with people in the passenger cars, I
was thinking that Tristram Gow ran the
ranch. Turns out, he had nothing to do with

the Bar DD, had his own spread north of the MacDunn range on Muddy Creek. He was a friend of Major MacDunn, being that they were both Scotsmen. In fact, they both hailed from Aberdeen, and Mr. Gow had agreed to head to Chicago and purchase the best three Angus bulls he could find, two for the Bar DD, the other for Mr. Gow's 7-3 Connected.

When we got off the train in Helena, there was a big crowd gathered. Not for us, of course. Folks had come to hear a bespectacled man from Dakota talk. That's how come I got to meet the President of the United States.

'Course, he wasn't the President then. I never would have expected him to amount to much myself.

He stood leaning against the big wooden column. Teddy Roosevelt addressed maybe a dozen cattlemen, businessmen, and one fellow I took to be an ink-slinger for the local newspaper because he kept furiously scribbling notes, trying to keep up with Teddy Roosevelt, and Teddy was a mighty fast talker.

"In the course of time, the great ranches will break up," Roosevelt told the listeners, his eager eyes squinting through his pince-nez.

"Smaller ranches, fenced in, with two hundred or three hundred cattle, can be managed more economically."

"Fenced?"

Me and Teddy Roosevelt looked at John Henry. Shoot, everybody give John Henry a stare. Nobody was used to hearing Teddy Roosevelt get interrupted.

"Fenced, sir. It is not an obscene word. It is the future."

"Who the hell are you, if you don't mind me asking?"

"Roosevelt, sir. Theodore Roosevelt. I own the Elk Horn . . . the Maltese Cross brand . . . along the Little Missouri in Medora over in Dakota Territory, although I embark for New York after these meetings. I have been asked to run as the Republican candidate for the mayor of New York City."

"You stringing wire in Dakota?" John Henry had something stuck in his craw. Me and Tommy knowed what it was.

"Sir." Roosevelt removed his glasses, and cleaned the lenses with a fine handkerchief. "If you missed my earlier comments, I precipitated them with the words 'in the course of time.' I have no idea when the right time will be, merely that at some point these vast ranges of this big, wonderful country must be fenced in. Your grass looks no better than the grass in Medora. The range is already strewn with dead cattle coming up the trail from Texas. We are facing one of the worst droughts in the history of the Northern Plains. In Montana, as well as in Dakota, in those creeks that still have water, I have found water so alkaline that even cattle dying of thirst refuse to drink it. Something must be done. *Progress* is not a filthy word."

John Henry had heard enough, and walked away. Me and Tommy started after our pard, but Mr. Gow stopped us, whispering: "Let us hear what else this man has to say." Well, we was drawing wages from Mr. Gow, and I saw John Henry duck inside a saloon, so I knew he wasn't going nowhere for a while. Later, Mr. Gow told us that Roosevelt had been the President of the Stockgrowers Association in Dakota, and had been sent as a representative at Montana's meeting of stockmen.

"Tell us about how you tracked down them thieves, Mister Roosevelt, hauled them back by yourself."

With a grin, he placed the glasses back atop his nose. "That story has made its way all the way to Helena?"

"Why didn't you just hang them?" another man asked. "That's what Gran Stuart and

William MacDunn would have done?"

A few men chuckled.

"Good men, both of them, but their methods are not mine."

"Didn't you read to 'em?" one man asked, and another fired right back: "Druther be hung myself!"

That caused a roar of laughter, and I don't think anybody laughed harder than Mr. Roosevelt.

"No, gentlemen, I read to stay awake. Alone, outnumbered three to one, I had to fight off sleep for forty hours, guarding them. But I had good company in Tolstoy."

"Tolstoy's a wonderful writer," Tommy said, and Mr. Roosevelt reached over to pat Tommy's shoulder, saying: "Bully for you, young man. Bully for you."

Someone brought out a mug of sarsaparilla from the saloon, and, while Mr. Roosevelt slaked his thirst, Mr. Gow said we'd best fetch John Henry, which is what we done. 'Course, by the time we come out of that saloon, Mr. Roosevelt, and the crowd, had gone.

After that, we walked to where they was holding our bulls in a pen, and Mr. Gow bought us some horses. John Henry got himself a big sorrel. Partial to sorrels, John

Henry was. Tommy threw his saddle on a black-faced grulla roan, and I picked out a garnet bay with a spider-web face. All of them was geldings, of course. Tommy called his horse Midnight Beauty, though I didn't think there was anything even pretty about that horse. John Henry never called his horses nothing, unless he was cussing them, except by the color, but I named mine Crabtown, because I never had much imagination when it came to naming horses. The watering hole across from the Sommer's Livery was called the Crabtown Saloon, which is where John Henry led us before we picked out our mounts.

We got fed in the Crabtown, too, because the bartender there served pickles, crackers, and sandwiches to patrons, and the food was free. Mr. Gow liked that. Nice guy, he was, but as big a skinflint as ever I worked for. Next, we got those horses I just mentioned. Old Man Sommer was shaking his head after he and Mr. Gow settled on a price, and we hit the trail, herding the three bulls right down Last Chance Gulch, and on out of town. Mr. Gow had a sorrel horse, too, bigger than John Henry's, and his was a stallion. He called him Champion.

But, I reckon you ain't interested in horses.

Took us five, six days to make it to the Bar DD, not forcing those bulls, because Angus bulls ain't ones to be hurried, and the range wasn't much to look at that summer. Not much good grass for those bulls, or our horses, to eat.

"Country'll be right pretty," John Henry said, "when it greens up."

"Aye," agreed Mr. Gow. Both of them sounded like they were trying to convince themselves of it.

That was about all the conversing anybody done, at least whilst me and Tommy was around. Now, Mr. Gow and John Henry talked some at night, or when they rode ahead of us, in whispers mostly, but would shut up whenever me and Tommy come close enough to hear. That was bothersome for Tommy. He didn't like secrets. I was too tuckered out to worry about it, and, besides, when John Henry had something to tell us, he'd tell us. Wasn't going to worry over his private conversations with Mr. Gow.

So, you figure it this way. I'd started out that spring skinning dead cattle in the Texas Panhandle, then worked as a muleskinner between Mobeetie and Dodge City. Then rode drag on a herd to Ogallala, and another outfit from Nebraska to Miles City. Then helped keep three black bulls company on a rollicking, stinking, noisy train all the way to Helena. And spent almost a week nursing those Angus doddies to the Bar DD ranch. I was tired.

John Henry laughed at me. Said: "You'll be able to sleep all winter."

Anyway, we got to the MacDunn Ranch, and it wasn't much to look at, either. I don't know. I guess I was mighty green in those days, no matter how grown-up I thought I was. I thought there'd be this real castle at the Bar DD headquarters. One of the books that Tommy had gotten from Jenks Fergus had been *The Lady of the Lake,* and Tommy would read some poems from it at nights on the trail. Even those muleskinners freighting for Captain Jonas admired Tommy's reading, because Tommy read real good. Well, *The Lady of the Lake* was about old Scotland, full of fights and heroes, and, well, naturally, I figured the ranch house would be like something Tommy described from that book.

We put the three bulls in an empty corral, and looked around. There were quite a few corrals, and a whopper of a barn, made of big logs chinked with mud. The main house was also a log cabin, with a dreary sod roof, just like the chuck house that stood between the MacDunn house and the bunkhouse.

71

Guess it was slightly better than some of the ranches we'd worked for in Texas, and a mite better than those sodbusters' places we'd seen in Nebraska. A four-seater privy, too, by thunder, tucked up underneath the hill rising behind the bunkhouse.

"What's that?" Tommy asked. I followed his finger to the lone building in a dip, partially hidden by a lean-to. Now, that building just didn't fit in with all the dirt-colored structures on the ranch. Some fool had taken whitewash to its plank boards, and it stood out among the weathered, brown grass. Looked brand-spanking new, until I got the opportunity to see it up close a short while later. That whitewash needed a fresh coat, let me tell you. The wind had beaten that paint and boards something fierce, so that, when you looked at it when you was near, it didn't appear to be no better than any of the ranch buildings. And me and Tommy got plenty of chances to see that house up closer than we — at least me — ever wanted to.

I figured it for a church. Boy, did I figure wrong.

"They put it up two years ago," said Mr. Gow, who was walking to the bunkhouse. "Come on, I want to introduce you to the boys. We'll get some coffee."

Boys was right. First one to race out of the bunkhouse wasn't even my age, and two other kids followed. What struck Tommy first was that nobody was in any hurry to come outside till after we got those three bulls penned. Maybe they hadn't heard us. The two stragglers couldn't catch that red-headed young 'un who was screaming — "Papa!" — and leaped into Mr. Gow's arms, almost knocking the Scotsman down. Me and Tommy didn't know what to make of that commotion. John Henry just grunted something, disappointed that his coffee would have to wait on account of some fool kid.

"Did you get the animals, Papa?" the red-headed boy asked, after a long hug and a kiss on the cheek.

"See for yourself." Mr. Gow pointed at the corral.

The boy didn't spend much time looking at the Angus beef, because me and Tommy took his attention. He just stared at us, didn't pay John Henry no mind, and looked back at his father.

"Can I help you drive ours back home?" he asked.

"You know the rules, Camdan," Mr. Gow said.

"But . . . Papa."

"No buts, Son." He squeezed his son's shoulder, and turned back to us, made the introductions.

Yeah, that was the first time I met Camdan Gow. He grew up, didn't he? Would have been thirteen back then, younger and shorter than me, but I was about to turn sixteen in another month or thereabouts. Well, I can't say I paid much attention to Camdan while his pa introduced us, because I was staring at the two boys who had come out of the bunkhouse behind Camdan Gow.

One of them wasn't no boy at all.

She had dark hair, and was wearing a red-checked blouse and duck pants. I couldn't recollect ever seeing pants on a girl before, but that was how she was dressed that day. Picture it plain as if it happened just yesterday.

"And, gentlemen," Mr. Gow said, "this is Lainie MacDunn and Walter Butler."

Lainie give us a curtsey. Walter, a big, strapping boy with close-cropped yellow hair, held out a big, strapping hand. I took it. He had a firm grip. Plus, he had better manners than Camdan Gow, I thought. Better manners than Tommy O'Hallahan, too, because Tommy didn't even offer to shake Walter's hand. On account he didn't see it, him staring at Lainie so. And, yes, sir, she was staring right back at him.

"No school today?" Mr. Gow asked.

"It's Sunday, Papa," Camdan replied.

"No church?"

"We read our scripture to Missus Blaire after breakfast," his son answered.

"And where are Blaire and William?"

"I am right here." A sprightly if stout woman followed that voice out of the chuck house. Her brown hair, just starting to gray, was tucked up in a bun. She busied herself wiping her hands on an apron, her face flushed, smiling, trying to fix her face as she walked toward us, wiping it with the hem of the apron after she had cleaned the flour off her hands. "I must look a mess, Tristram. Trying to make sourdough biscuits for supper. Good heavens, I did not expect you back for two or three days."

Her accent was straight out of Sir Walter Scott, too.

"I left Chicago as soon as I could. Saw no need dallying around there, Blaire." Mr. Gow kissed her cheek, and Mrs. MacDunn stepped back. They seemed to be admiring one another.

"Can we see the bulls?" Lainie MacDunn asked.

"Lainie!"

Let me tell you this — Mrs. MacDunn

75

could scowl with the best of them. Back in those days, that wasn't a question befitting a proper girl — you didn't even say bull in front of a lady — but I figured any girl who wore duck trousers wasn't proper.

"Lass," Mr. Gow said, "I promised these young lads they could have coffee first. I dare say they've earned it, and maybe a bowl of your mother's delicious pudding. Blaire MacDunn, these fine cowmen are John Henry Kenton, Tommy O'Hallahan, and Jim Hawkins."

"Jim Hawkins?" That took Lainie's attention away from Angus bulls or Tommy O'Hallahan. She sized me up right quickly. "With an i-n or an e-n?"

I didn't know what to say. Wasn't sure I heard right, or what it mattered, or maybe I was just flummoxed to have to try to converse with a girl, a real pretty girl, who wore pants.

"I-n." It was Tommy who answered. "H-a-w-k-i-n-s."

Well, my ears started burning red again. "I can spell my own name, Tommy," I told him, and that was true. Ma had learned me my ABCs, and, while I couldn't read real good — all right, I couldn't read hardly nothing at all — I knew how to sign my own name, even though I made the J and S

76

backwards, and my K always turned out crooked.

"Is that true?" Lainie asked.

Now, I was really mad. "Yes, ma'am. I can spell my own name. J-i-m. That's short for James, but nobody ever calls me James. H-a-. . . ."

"Not that, you dumb oaf."

"Lainie MacDunn!" her mother snapped.

"I don't care if he can read or write, Mother," Lainie said. By that time, John Henry was shuffling his feet, wondering if he'd ever get his coffee. "I just wanted to know how he spelled his name. It's Jim Hawkins, Mother, just like. . . ."

"You apologize to Master Hawkins at once, Lainie." Mrs. MacDunn was nobody to trifle with when she got riled, and her daughter had riled her. Looked like everyone was getting riled, because I was plumb ready to thrash Tommy for embarrassing me so. "You do not insult our guest, young lady!"

Lainie drew a deep breath, let it out, and stared at me, but I didn't see no forgiveness in her eyes as she told me: "I'm sorry I called you a dumb oaf, Jim Hawkins." She extended her right hand, and now it was Tommy who was getting riled at me. Because I got to touch Lainie MacDunn first.

Yes, boy, that was the first time I met your grandma. To tell you the truth, on that day, I kind of hoped I'd never see that irksome girl again.

CHAPTER EIGHT

No argument about it — Mrs. MacDunn was a good cook. She let us sample her sucamagrowl, about as tasty and sweet a pudding as ever I ate. But they used Folgers at the Bar DD, and me and Tommy had grown accustomed to Arbuckles' coffee. Folgers didn't put a stick of peppermint in its can, so I figured it would be hard for Mrs. MacDunn to get any help from us cowboys since she couldn't bribe us none with a piece of candy. That's because I hadn't met Major MacDunn yet.

"Where is William?" Mr. Gow asked.

"The gather," she said. "I do not know when he shall return."

Mr. Gow gave her a large envelope. "Here are the bills of sale, and a detailed invoice for the amount he owes me. Alas, we underestimated the expense not only of those three animals, but the price of everything in Chicago. He may pay me when next we meet. And I picked up a book, which might interest both you and William."

She tore open that envelope, pulling out a book, leaving the papers alone, gasping and giving Mr. Gow the most fetching look of appreciation, till he announced: "I must take my leave after we eat."

"But, Papa!" Camdan cried out, him looking as hurt as Mrs. MacDunn. "You just got here."

"Aye, but we are gathering cattle, too. Work, lad. There's always work."

"I wish you could stay, Tristram," Mrs. MacDunn said. "Company is so rare in this country."

Later, when we was in the barn alone, that comment set Tommy off, her complaining about the lack of company, when me and Tommy and John Henry was standing right there.

Sadly Mr. Gow shook his head, and offered Mrs. MacDunn a comforting smile.

We ate our chuck, drunk our coffee, outside, it being warm. And windy. Wind picked up, had no plans of relenting. I noticed Tommy kept making eyes at Lainie, while Camdan Gow busied himself trying to size up us newcomers. Then Mr. Gow said he needed to ride back to his ranch, told John Henry they'd best get a move on.

Me and Tommy tossed our dirty dishes into the wreck pan, tipped our hats at Mrs. Mac-Dunn, and started to follow our pard, but he turned around, holding up his hand. Had this funny look on his face, kept moving his lips around like he was trying to think of something to say. So Mr. Gow said it for him.

"You shall be staying here, laddies."

"We ride with John Henry," Tommy said. Defiant. Like he had expected this sort of ambuscade all along. That's when I figured out what John Henry and Mr. Gow had been conspiring all along on the drive up from Helena. My ears started burning once more.

"Ain't no job for you two at the Seven-Three Connected," John Henry finally said. "There is one for you here."

"But. . . ." That's as far as I got.

"Gow's hired me," John Henry said. "Big gather's still going on up there. That's where I'll be working the rest of this summer. You two boys got a job here."

"That's the first I've heard about it," Tommy snapped back.

"It is the truth," Mrs. MacDunn said. She sounded kind of sad. "You boys are most welcome here."

"Reckon we'll still ride with you," Tommy said.

"There's no job for you." This time John Henry spoke sharply.

"Maybe Mister Gow isn't hiring," Tommy argued. "There are other outfits that way."

"Or we can ride the grubline," I added.

"Use your heads!" John Henry put his hands on his hips, maybe to keep from knocking us with his fists, and Mrs. Mac-Dunn shooed the other boys and Lainie back toward the bunkhouse. "We're new to this country. That's why we're splitting up. It ain't permanent. You see what the Bar DD's like, I'll check out Gow's ranch, and them other outfits working up yonder. You do your job here, maybe I can hire on come winter. If anybody's hiring then. If we all get let go, which is mighty likely, we'll have a good idea about what ranches to visit. So we don't starve all winter. We need to learn about Montana, is all. This summer, we'll all be getting an education." He winked at Mr. Gow.

"The MacDunn Ranch is the biggest on the Sun River range," Mr. Gow said, trying to sell us on this plan. "You will not find better employers than William and Blaire. Fear not, laddies. I will return John Henry to you in fine form. And maybe I can hire you on next spring. My ranch is growing, and with that outstanding Aberdeen Angus specimen down there, it shall grow even more."

I looked for Tommy to say something. He thought for a spell, started to ask a question, then stopped. Knew it was hopeless, that everything had been decided long ago. John Henry took that as the signing of our peace treaty, so he turned away, and walked to the corral with Mr. Gow. Just like that, he was gone, leaving me and Tommy alone with a bunch of strangers. We left for the bunkhouse, as Mrs. MacDunn stood in front of the chuck house watching Mr. Gow and John Henry push the black bull over the hills.

Our beds was what we called "Montana feathers" — just hay on boards — about as comfortable as rocks. The log walls kept most of the wind out, although the Mac-Dunns had knocked the chinking out to allow some wind to pass through. Good thing, too. That was turning out to be one hot summer.

Bunkhouse was practically empty. Most of the Bar DD hands was on their big summer gather — roundup, you call it — which is where I figured we'd be come next morning, but it turned out Mrs. MacDunn had another plan for us. John Henry had known about that, too, from all his conspiring with Mr. Gow. Ringing that cast-iron triangle next morn, Mrs. MacDunn kept hollering at us to hurry, else we'd be late for school.

School!

Walter Butler and Camdan Gow giggled like girls when we come out of the bunkhouse. Thought it was some mighty funny joke.

It being warm again, even with the sun barely up, we ate in silence, then followed Mrs. MacDunn to that white building. Saw some other kids walking, or riding, over the hill, filing into that whitewashed building that wasn't no church at all.

"Class," she said as everybody but me and Tommy sat down in his or her desk, "we have two new students joining us for the rest of the school year. Please give Tommy O'Hallahan and Jim Hawkins a hearty Montana Territory welcome."

On account of the warmth, Mrs. Mac-Dunn had left the door and windows open, so, hat in hand, I shot a glance at the door behind me.

Through clenched mouth, Tommy whispered: "Don't you dare run out on me, Hawkins."

Every kid in that schoolhouse greeted us, not too enthusiastic, with hellos and howdies, and then I told Mrs. MacDunn that I had hired on as a cowhand, not to go to some school. I also heard the sound of horses, lots of them, over toward the ranch. That sound sure interested me more than any schooling.

"And you will work, Jim," she said firmly. "After school. That's the law."

"Law?"

Tommy wasn't no help. He just stared ahead, and he wasn't even looking at Lainie. Probably wasn't seeing anything.

"Three years ago," Mrs. MacDunn said, "the territorial legislature enacted a compulsory school attendance law."

I wasn't sure what that meant, but I told her that in Texas and Indiana, they didn't hold school in summers on account of all the work to be done. 'Course, I hadn't really boned up on the school laws, but I thought it was true.

Mrs. MacDunn had a pleasant laugh. "Well, this is Montana, and our school break is during winter. As I said, Jim, you will work. On Saturdays, and every day *after* school. Shall we get started?"

I wasn't finished yet. "I don't see how come me and Tommy is here while John

Henry ain't. I can sign my own name. John Henry has to make a big old X. Granted, he puts a lot of flourish in that mark, but he's the one that needs schooling. Not us."

"Excellent," she said. "I wish Mister Kenton were here, too, but the law does not require adults attend school, just children. Let's see." Leaving us standing there, she picked up a writing tablet, and called out a bunch of names, the boys and girls answering — "Here" or "Present." — while me and Tommy stood between the American flag and a picture of President Cleveland like a couple of cads. Next, she put down the tablet, picked up a book, and planted herself between me and Tommy.

"Class," she said, "Mister Gow yesterday brought a fascinating book that we shall use to practice our reading. At the same time, this book will educate us on the wonders of what most of your parents do, and that is ranching." She held up the book for all to see. "It is titled *Cattle-Raising on the Plains of North America,* written by Walter Baron von Ritchofen, presently of Colorado, although he is a native of Prussia, and published only last year." She smiled. That lady had a lovely smile. "This book reminds me of a similar one authored by James Brisbin. Mister Brisbin's book, *The Beef Bo-*

86

nanza, with its glorious subtitle, *How to Get Rich on the Plains,* lured Major MacDunn, Lainie, and me to America." She opened the book, and handed it to Tommy.

"Tommy, please read the first paragraph."

The kids, all except Lainie, just sniggered while Tommy took the book in his trembling hands. Mrs. MacDunn pretended like she didn't hear. Maybe she didn't. I don't know why Tommy was acting scared, but I knew why those other kids was giggling. They pegged us as a couple of yacks. Well, Tommy showed them.

" 'No doubt,' " Tommy began, " 'some of my older readers will remember that when as boys they studied the geography of America, they were taught that all the land west of the Missouri River was barren and worthless, and that it would forever remain so. It was known that it was the abode of Indians and wild beasts; that the buffalo roamed over its vast plains; and it commonly bore the name of "The Great American Desert." ' "

No, sir, there wasn't no giggling being done then. The kids had fallen real quiet, and Mrs. MacDunn just stood there, amazed. She took the book, her eyes just blooming, and said: "Fantastic. Utterly fantastic, Thomas." Reckon she didn't think

87

Tommy was befitting a name for a boy who read so fine. "Here, take a seat behind Richard there."

Tommy hesitated, because Mrs. Mac-Dunn had give me the baron's book, and my mouth went as dry Mobeetie in the summer. My pard wanted to stay with me, help me, maybe whisper the words to me, somehow, but Mrs. MacDunn shooed him to his desk.

"Go on, Jim," she instructed me, looking lovely, expecting me — since I had done told her how good I could sign my own name — to read as fantastic as Tommy O'Hallahan. "Read the second paragraph."

I looked down at that book in my own shaking hands.

"Go ahead, Jim."

I wet my lips.

She pointed to the second paragraph. I spied the first word. It was a big one. Can't recollect what exactly it was, but it started with a G. Funny, ain't it? I remember the first paragraph that Tommy read so well, but that's all I recollect from that book. I read it later. Bunch of lies, most of it. Maybe not lies, but cattle raising wasn't no sure bet, and that's what the baron and that Mr. Brisbin preached to everyone.

I warrant you have to memorize the Pledge

of Allegiance. We didn't have that when I was in school. Your mama, when she was your age, I remember her having to learn something from the Declaration of Independence or the Constitution, both of them, I think, maybe a Bible verse or two. In that summer of 1886, though, Mrs. Blaire Mac-Dunn had us all memorizing the first paragraph of *Cattle-Raising on the Plains of North America.* So it got burned into my brain, and, eventually, I could read it, too. Not as good as Tommy, but I could read it.

But not that first morning.

I looked at them letters, at that big word, then I lifted my head. Everyone stared at me, everyone but Tommy. He wouldn't, couldn't. Just set his eyes on his boots, embarrassed for me.

"Go on, Jim," Mrs. MacDunn coaxed, and I shamed myself.

That's what galls me, to this day. I burst out in tears, bawling like a kid. Shamed. Then, shame made way for anger, and I hurled that book across the room, near about tore off Camdan Gow's head, and I run as fast as I could out of that schoolhouse.

CHAPTER NINE

I run straight into the hands of a mighty big man.

Rough hands gripped my arms tight, me squirming, kicking, snapping at him to let me go, but blinded by tears so I couldn't see straight. He kept saying things like: "Hold on there, young man!" Scottish accent, of course. Sounded like everybody on Montana's Front Range come from Scotland. Finally he give up on trying to shake any sense into me, calm me down, deciding I'd pretty soon nail his shins with the toes of my boots, and he threw me hard to the ground. "Stay there!" His voice sounded like thunder.

"William," Mrs. MacDunn said with a start. "Leave him. . . ." Her voice cracked; she couldn't finish.

Well, I started to my feet, my eyes clearing, and I saw him. Looked to stand about twelve feet tall, caked in dust and grime, plaid trousers tucked in stovepipe boots, and a big gray hat setting low on his forehead. 'Course, he wasn't twelve feet tall, but he stood a good four inches over six feet. Big shoulders, broad chest, and muscles in his arms straining to tear his blue cotton shirt to nothing but threads. That giant, Major William Bruce MacDunn, turned to gather the reins of a blood bay gelding grazing just behind him.

"What is going on here, Lainie?" the major asked his wife. "Who is this little hellion?"

"He is just upset, William. A new student. A new hand for us."

The reins dropped back to the ground, and Major MacDunn turned, glaring at his wife now. He grunted something, took a step or two toward the schoolhouse, stopped, and give me another look before giving his wife an even harder look.

"Where's Gow?"

"Tristram returned to his ranch. You have seen the two Angus he-cows?"

"Aye, I did. Hardee, Ish, and I brought in some new mounts. When did Gow leave?"

"Yesterday. He stayed just long enough to eat."

"And deposit yet another orphan!"

Well, I snapped right back at him, "I ain't

no . . . !" Then I got smart enough to shut my trap. Let them think I was an orphan. If they learned that I was nothing but a runaway, they might send me back to Vigo County, Indiana, and I had no hankering to take up farming.

"Two, William," Mrs. MacDunn said softly, her eyes shining. "I don't think either is older than fourteen."

Reckon we looked younger to her, but age didn't make no difference to the major.

"When I was fourteen years old," he said, "I was. . . ."

"Yes, William," she said, still gentle. "I know. We could use the help, and they are both hard workers."

The major glowered. He was looking at me again. "But not such good students."

"He's young. Embarrassed. 'Twas my fault, not his, William. I did not understand the circumstances."

He stepped right up to me, staring down with the meanest blue eyes. Like looking up into two blue gun barrels. Felt like I was staring up into a big bronze statue. "And what name do you go by?"

"Jim Hawkins," I told him.

"All right, Hawkins. Get back to school. We shall see how good a cowhand you are *after* school."

Let me tell you, I hadn't calmed down none. My ears was still aflame, and I'd never had the good sense not to jump into a fight, even when there was no way I'd ever win. So I told Major MacDunn that there was no way I was going back into that stupid white building with that teacher. Only I didn't call her a teacher. Still seeing red and feeling nothing but hate, I called her a vile, savage name. Next thing I knew, the major had knocked me to the ground, loosened a tooth, split both lips, and busted my nose. He done all that with just one, backhanded swing.

"William!" his wife screamed.

Spitting out blood, and rage, I scrambled to my feet, and ran as fast as I could for the barn.

"Come back here!" the big man bellowed, and he started after me, for another pound of flesh, I warrant, and likely would have gotten it and then some, only Mrs. Mac-Dunn could yell as loud as he could, and with just as much force. She barked out his name again, and the major stopped.

I didn't.

Quick as I could, I gathered up Crabtown in the corral, led him to the barn, found the tack. Had no intention of going to the

93

bunkhouse to get my possibles. Didn't amount to much, nohow. Give no thought to my bunky, Tommy O'Hallahan, either. He could find me if he wanted. I aimed to ride hard and fast, maybe to Miles City if I could find it, get me a job there. For the life of me, I couldn't figure out why John Henry didn't try to hire on there when we first got to Montana. Plenty of outfits that way. Plenty of Texicans. Wasn't sure where I'd end up, but I was through with the Bar DD.

Got the bridle on, blanket, then the saddle — didn't even bother grooming the gelding first — that's how riled I was — and had just started to tie off the latigo when this voice, quiet-like, said behind me: "You can't do this."

"You just watch me," I told Lainie Mac-Dunn without so much as giving her a glance.

"It isn't your horse," she said, and that give me pause.

My saddle — same soap saddle I'd been riding for years — my blanket, my bridle, but she was right as rain. Mr. Gow had bought us those mounts, and I figured the price was included in that invoice he had left behind for Major MacDunn. Well, I muttered an oath, but, like I say, I was mad, so I told her, looking at her this time: "Your pa can come after me if he wants." If I owned a six-shooter, I would have patted it — just like some villain today in one of them moving-picture shows.

"You wouldn't want that, Jim Hawkins," she says. "Two years ago, my father and Granville Stuart met in Helena, and decided to put an end to horse thieves and cattle rustlers." She traced a finger across her pretty throat. "They hanged so many, they became known as the Montana Stranglers." She must have thought that was funny, because she let out a little giggle. "The Montana Stock Growers Association voted Granville Stuart president and my father vice president in appreciation of all their hard work. I should hate to see you stretched from a wagon tongue, Jim Hawkins."

I started to lead Crabtown out of the barn, but Lainie MacDunn stood in front of me.

"Listen," she said, "I'm sorry. I'm sorry I called you an oaf yesterday. I'm sorry my father hit you. A violent temper he has." She handed me a calico rag, and my hand reached out and took it, because I couldn't control my own limbs, and wiped the blood off my face.

"What brought you to Montana?" she asked.

"A string of horses," I snapped back, then felt bad about it. "I don't know," I heard myself saying softly. "John Henry said we're going to Montana, so we went, me and Tommy. Things was bad in Texas. Was a hard winter."

"It's been mild here," she said. "Just perfect."

"You need some rain." I kept telling myself to get out of there, mount up, kick my horse into a high lope, but there I was, bloody rag in one hand, reins in another, and I was asking Lainie: "Why'd you settle here?"

"Like Mother said . . . a book. A book about how wonderful cattle ranching is in the United States territories. When the Dee and Don bought out the Donovan and Marshall Ranches, Father was appointed the overseer. He knew cattle, especially his Angus, and he had served in the army with several men on the board. So we set sail for America. I was sick of Scotland anyway. That's part of it. The other. . . ." Her eyes started to tear, but she forced shook her head, smiling again. "But . . . we wouldn't be here if not for Brisbin's book."

I could hear folks outside, knew I had blown my chance of escaping.

Lainie held a book in her left hand.

"Is that the book?" I asked.

"No." She smiled. "This is a much better book. That's why I asked you how you spell your name, Jim Hawkins. And it's i-n, just like this book." She held it out to me. I didn't give a fip about no book, but I did like hearing her talk, watching her eyes shine. I didn't feel so angry anymore.

"I first read it in Aberdeen . . . oh my goodness, four or five years ago, I imagine. It appeared in *Young Folks* magazine, and later was printed as a book. It's about pirates and mutiny and buried gold. It's a corker of a story by Robert Louis Stevenson . . . *Treasure Island.* And the hero of the tale is a young lad named Jim Hawkins."

"Well. . . ." I had nothing else to say.

"Well," she finished for me, "Mother thinks we're foolish kids, but we're practically grown up. Still, we cannot revolt. At least, I cannot. Mother needs to teach, and boys. . . ." There were those tears again, but just like that they vanished, on account of Lainie wouldn't let herself turn sad. "Were I a schoolteacher," she said, "I'd teach my students something they'd enjoy. Not books about ranching. Not that foolishness in a *McGuffey's Reader.* Not Byron."

"Oh, Tommy likes Lord Byron." I heard myself saying it, calling Tommy by his name, and just couldn't stop myself. "Recites his poems a lot."

"Does he?" She looked over her shoulder, then back at me. "Where is Tommy?"

"He knows better than get in my way," I said, and didn't quite have the guts to tell her: "Unlike you."

"What's he like?" she asked. My stomach knotted, but, just as quick, she was shaking her head hard, saying: "No, no, no, I should not have asked that. What . . . well, I can help you learn to read, Tommy."

I didn't correct her, tell her my name was Jim, not Tommy. I just handed her the bloody rag, thanked her, and started to go, but now somebody else blocked my path, and I knew I couldn't run over Major Mac-Dunn.

"Lainie," he said, kind of quiet for him, "go back to school. I shall attend to Master Hawkins."

Well, she knew better than to argue. She mouthed the words: "Please stay, Jim," — not Jim Hawkins, just Jim — and turned and walked past her father.

I got ready for another thrashing, but I aimed to whip him of the habit of whipping me.

"Fine-looking gelding you have there," he said.

"Yes," I said, and knew to add, "sir."

"You have a bill of sale?"

"Just wanted to see how my saddle fit his back," I told him, and turned to take off the saddle. I'd carry my gear with me all the way to Miles City, all the way to Texas if need be. I didn't need a horse. It wasn't the way a real cowboy would think. A real cowboy wouldn't walk across the street. But . . . I was mad.

Major MacDunn did something then that I never would have expected him to do in ten thousand years. He laughed. Laughed hard and loud, slapped his thigh, and come to me, helped me get that saddle off, and then he slapped Crabtown's rear, let the horse run into the yard.

"You and I got off on the wrong foot, Jim," he said. "There's a job here, but school is part of that job. I expect all of my hands to read and write. Educated men are better men. So you will attend school. But not today."

I give him an inquisitive look.

"There are horses in the corral," he said, "that need the rough ridden off them. I understand from your saddle pal that you're the best bronc' rider he has ever known. Better even than this John Henry Kenton he talks so much about."

Him and Tommy must have had quite the conversation before he come to the barn.

"So you'll break horses the rest of today," he said. "You'll follow Eugene Hardee's orders without fail. He's my foreman. But school starts again in the morning, and you will follow Missus MacDunn's orders. Without fail." He held out a big right hand, practically swallowing mine when I took it.

"There is another thing," he told me. "You will apologize to Missus MacDunn at supper tonight. You will never use profane language in front of her again, and certainly will never call her anything disrespectful. For if you do, I will ignore your youth, and kill you."

CHAPTER TEN

So I stayed.

I should tell you a thing or two about Gene Hardee and Ish Fishtorn. For the first week or so I spent at the Bar DD, working with them two waddies gave me the gumption to stick with that school. Good cowhands, the both of them, and good horsemen. Ish's real name was Lyman. Folks called him Ish, I guess, because he didn't want to be called Lyman.

As far as Major MacDunn, he wasn't so easy to get to know. Or like. Or understand. He'd be almost human one moment, then turn hard as granite the next, like that time in the barn, when just a few minutes after he had laughed at something I'd said, he threatened to kill me if I called his wife a foul name. Am fairly certain he meant it, too. Wasn't some idle threat. Major Mac-Dunn brings to mind one of those horses I broke, or tried to break, on that first week at the Bar DD. A little dapple gray gelding that became part of my string who I took to calling Gray Boy. Had the smoothest gait of any horse I ever rode, but Gray Boy would test you, yes, sir. Start to relax, and he'd start to bucking, like he knew when you wasn't ready.

Once, when I thought I'd ridden him to a standstill, then had him doing some turns, stops, backing up, got him going in a little trot, worked him till he was good and tired, I reined in, let him catch his wind, and I was taking off my hat to wipe the sweat off my brow. Next thing I know, I'm spread-eagled on the ground, fighting for my own breath, eyes blinded by the dust Gray Boy's kicking up. Ish and Hardee had to drag me out of the corral before I got stomped to death.

"That's a mean horse," Ish said. "I'd trade him for a busted watch."

"You don't know him like I do," I told Ish. "He's a good horse . . . just. . . ." I watched Gray Boy stop at the far side of the corral, tossing his head like he was telling me that he was the boss of this outfit. "Just . . . notional."

See, that was the difference between the major and Gray Boy. The horse I could savvy, him being a free-spirited animal, kind of like me and John Henry. But Major Mac-Dunn, him I didn't ever know what he was thinking, or why.

Saturdays were my favorite. No surprise there, I reckon. No school. No church. I'd saddle up Gray Boy or Crabtown, maybe some shavetail mare, and get to do what I'd come to Montana to do.

By then, the gather was all but done, but Hardee told me not to fret too much, that the fall gather would start up before too long, and I'd get my fill of working cattle.

"Lot of cattle," I said.

"Too damn' many," Gene said.

I picture that day, hot as blazes, the two of us atop a hill, just watching the dust, as Tommy and Ish rode around a mud hole that was rapidly losing its mud. Getting baked dry, I mean. Gene was right, too, about the cattle. Most of them were Mac-Dunn's Angus, but he had plenty of long-horns, too, a lot of them brought up the trail that summer, and looked about as skinny and weak as the cattle I'd seen in Miles City.

Having hooked a leg over the horn, Hardee sat atop his big gelding while he softened a mouthful of tobacco, waiting for me to do some fixing on my stirrup. I still owned that soap saddle of mine, and it wasn't the best-built slick fork a cowboy ever owned. Hardee spit, turned, and, watching me do some good rigging with latigo laces, he just shook his head, saying: "You're a rawhide like all them other Texicans."

"Rather be a rawhide than a sagebrush man," I answered, but looked up with a grin just so he'd know I didn't really mean no insult.

That's what it was like, back then. Ask any Montana cowpuncher, and he'd tell you Texas cowboys were nothing but rawhides, misers who'd fix anything with leather. Put that question the other way around, and a Texican would let you know that Montanans didn't know a thing about nothing except sagebrush.

It was all in good fun. Most times.

Ish and Tommy had ridden up just as Hardee was telling me: "Well, at least you ain't no knock-kneed Oregonian sumbitch."

To which Ish Fishtorn said: "Watch it, Gene. I happen to be a knock-kneed Oregonian sumbitch."

We all chuckled at that, and I swung up into the saddle, which caused Hardee to clap with mocking approval, said he didn't think my rigging would hold. I told him I was good at making things last, and, sighing, Ish said: "Wish you could make a water hole last." He pointed at the mud.

"Ain't good," Hardee said.

"Gotta rain sometime," Tommy said.

"Ain't gotta do nothin'." Hardee spit again, put his boots back in the stirrups, and eased his horse toward a battered old cottonwood tree — only shade there was for miles — at the edge of that dried-up mud hole. He leaned over, started feeling the bark, eventually even pulled out his pocket knife, and cut away at it. I thought he might be carving his name or something in the trunk, but he didn't make any letters, and finally folded the blade, and slipped the knife back into his vest pocket.

"You thinking about becoming a lumberjack?" Ish Fishtorn teased him.

Our foreman wasn't in the mood to be funning. He pointed at the tree. "Bark's mighty thick," he said.

"Won't be for long," Ish said, "if we don't get some rain."

With a sigh, Gene Hardee rode away from the cottonwood, and pointed at the cattle. "Let's push them boys over toward the creek, see if they can find some better grass down that way."

We rode toward the Bar DD beef.

■ ■ ■ ■

Saturdays were a lot funner, though, I imagine, for Tommy. He spent a lot of time, mostly of evenings after supper, walking about the ranch yard with Lainie. She spent some time with me, too.

You ever read *Treasure Island*? Good book. I liked it a whole lot more than I did anything else Mrs. MacDunn had us read in school. I could picture myself as the Jim Hawkins in that story. Once she was done with her hand-holding, cooing, and grinning with Tommy, Lainie would venture back to the bunkhouse, where she'd sit with me a spell. She worked as my tutor, same as John Henry and ofttimes Tommy, and Hardee and Ish did, practicing with me, reading with me, things like that. Mostly, she read *Treasure Island* to me. Good book, like I said. Smelled nice, too. Lainie. Not the book.

After a couple of weeks, I wasn't so flabbergasted over Lainie MacDunn. Sometimes, when the reading and lessons were over, we'd sit out by the bunkhouse, talking a mite. Nice times, watching the horses in the corral snort and frolic, liking the wind as it cooled things off.

"What was Aberdeen like?" I asked her one evening.

"Old," she said, and laughed.

"What did it look like?"

"Old." She laughed again.

"Well, what did folks do there?"

"Fishing. Shipbuilding. The two Ds in our Father's brand stand for the Dee and Don Rivers of Aberdeen."

"I knew that already," I told her. Didn't want her to think I was ignorant. Tommy had told me that before, and, if I knew anything, it was whose brand I was riding for. The Dee & Don Rivers Land and Cattle Company, Incorporated.

"Old," she said, "but not primitive. Like here. We had a sewer system and gas lights."

"A sewer system!" We looked at each other funny.

"Yes."

"I ain't talking to no girl about sewers, Lainie MacDunn," I told her. "Even if she does wear pants."

She reached out, eyes twinkling — you'd think it was love, but it was her cussed mischievousness — and gently touched my hand. My instinct was to jerk back like her fingers were a rattler's fangs, but I just gripped the handle of that rawhide rocker tighter, till I got comfortable with the notion.

"And what is it you'd like to talk about, Jim Hawkins?"

Didn't have an answer for her. Too scared. I just stared out ahead, swallowed, and jutted my jaw out toward her mother. She stood at the top of the hill behind the house, wind just whipping her dress, practically blowing her down.

"Well?" Lainie asked. She hadn't noticed her ma, though she knew Mrs. MacDunn was up there. That lady was always up there, every evening. Reminded me of a coyote that used to hang out in front of the bunkhouse at the Ladder 3E back in Texas. Hung out there every night, staring, like he was wondering what we did in that place, almost like he was a pet. I started to get used to him being there. Till John Henry shot it dead with his Winchester.

"What's your ma doing there every night?" I asked.

The smile blew asunder. No more twinkles in her eye, and her hand went to her waist, as she sat rigid. "Thinking," she said stiffly.

"About what?" I asked.

"My brothers."

Then Lainie was gone. Nary a good bye. Nothing. She just up and left me sitting in front of the bunkhouse, made a beeline for her home.

"Her brothers died," Tommy told me later that evening.

"She told you that?" I asked.

"Of course, she told me that," he snapped. "I didn't just make it up. She talks to me a lot more than she talks to you, and we're not always talking about Long John Silver or what sounds a C makes."

That riled me considerable, but I bit my tongue, and shoved my clenched fists deep in my pockets.

"How'd they die?" I asked.

"They drowned."

We were getting ready for bed, Tommy sitting on his bunk, pulling off his boots, me just standing there with my hands in my pockets, and looking like that coyote after John Henry shot him the first time. Kind of surprised, unbelieving, hurt, all at the same time. Tommy grinned, because he knew something I didn't.

"The oldest brother got in trouble in the river. The younger one jumped in to save him, but Tavish . . . he's the young one . . . couldn't swim a lick, and they both drowned. That happened when Lainie was thirteen. That's the real reason why the

MacDunns left Scotland. Oh, they knew Mister Gow . . . he'd been up here for more than a decade . . . and after Simon and Tavish died, the major wanted to put Scotland behind him. He has. So has Lainie. I don't think you could say the same about Blaire. That's why she teaches school, why she runs this bunkhouse like an orphanage. She wants her two sons back." His grin widened. "Lainie didn't tell you that, eh?"

I wet my lips. Looking back, I realized at first I'd been jealous that my pard, my best friend and bunky, good old Tommy O'Hallahan was spending more time with Lainie MacDunn than he spent with me. Now me and Lainie hadn't gotten off to a good start, what with her riling me so, but she'd become my friend, too. Likely the first friend who was a girl I'd ever had. I never counted that old red-haired fat woman in Mobeetie who kept telling me she'd never had a friend as good as me, her being roostered eight days a week, and a whore to boot.

Right then, when Tommy was giving me this look, pleased to be telling me something, and even happier to know his words were stinging me good, I knew Tommy was jealous of me. Shucks, I spent maybe twenty minutes with Lainie on Saturday evenings, and a few minutes after school. That's all. Lainie sat across from Tommy in the schoolhouse, while I was stuck between some freckle-faced boy whose name I've long forgotten and Camdan Gow. Lainie stayed as close to Tommy as my butt stayed to the saddle.

"I reckon we talk about other things," I said, and Tommy's face turned red. Hadn't meant nothing by it. It was the truth, is all.

Tommy hit me first, a real chicken-livered thing to do, me with both hands in my pockets, and I somersaulted over my bunk, and fell to the floor. Tommy let out a curse, and dived right after me. I remember hearing Camdan Gow yell: "Fight!" Next thing, I knew, I was on my feet, fists swinging wildly, Tommy grunting, getting in some good punches. I tasted blood. Couldn't see a thing, blinded by tears, but I could tell I was doing my share of damage.

"Go get him, Texas!"

"Kick his butt, Hawkins!"

"Stay in there!"

"Use your left, Tommy!"

Only us boys filled the bunkhouse. Gene Hardee had ridden off to oversee a herd coming up from Nebraska, and Ish was the only grown-up man, other than the major, who was at the ranch that night, but Ish must have been in the barn or privy or somewhere.

I busted Tommy's nose wide open. Knew that because I heard Camdan Gow say so. Then we both were on the floor, kicking. Tommy was trying his best to get his thumbs into my eyeballs, with me holding him off, but growing weaker. Maybe we would have killed each other if Ish hadn't busted through the door.

"Fire!" he yelled first. Then: "What the hell's going on here?" He didn't wait for any explanation, he was shoving through, tossing Camdan Gow one way, Walter Butler another. My eyes started to clear, and I focused on Tommy's enraged face. Behind him appeared Ish, who jerked Tommy off me, and threw him like he was nothing but a canvas war bag. Threw him toward the door.

"Get up!" Ish was yelling at all of us boys. "And get out. We got a prairie fire to put out."

CHAPTER ELEVEN

Didn't see raging blazes, no smoke, just a small woman, a stranger, standing next to Mrs. MacDunn, and a Negro cowhand, who had driven the spring wagon. He was switching out the lathered team. She stood weaving, fanning her face, talking excitedly to Mrs. MacDunn.

"Mother!" Camdan Gow sprinted ahead of me, and wrapped his arms around that tall, frail spectacle of a female. Almost knocked her down. "What is it, Mother?"

"Prairie fire." She looked past her son and at the major, who just stepped out of the house, throwing fancy leather braces over his shoulders. "You've got to help us. Please help us. I've ridden. . . ."

I reckon she was about to collapse from the strain of it all, because Mrs. MacDunn took her, helped her toward the house.

"Where?" the major asked.

"North of Old Agency," she said.

The major turned. "Fishtorn, get these boys mounted. All of them."

"Not Camdan!" Mrs. Gow pleaded, but her son wouldn't have none of that. He told her he was going, and the major agreed.

"We must all go. Tristram will need every hand he can get, dry and windy as it is. Blaire, you and Lainie. . . ."

"We are going, too," Mrs. MacDunn told him. Yes, she was the only person I ever met who could make the major back down.

Rode all night, we did, taking advantage of a half moon, but even before dawn we could smell burning grass. Our eyes started to sting. At the Gow Ranch, we fortified ourselves with coffee, and, it being daylight by then, Mrs. MacDunn noticed my face, swollen, bruised, caked with dried blood.

"My goodness, Jim," she said. "What happened to you?"

"I run into something at the bunkhouse," I said. That wasn't enough, so I explained further: "It being dark and all."

At first, she halfway believed me, but Tommy stood just a few rods behind me, and, when she spotted his smashed lips and that shiner I'd given him, she asked: "Did you run into the same thing, Tommy?"

"Just about," he said, which got Walter

114

Butler to giggling like a girl.

The major ordered the girls to stay behind at the ranch, then led the rest of us to the fire, but not before he gave the girls one last order: "If the fire gets too close, get into the root cellar. Do not try to outrun it. You will die if you do."

Never seen a prairie fire, have you, boy? Pray to God you never do. Like you're standing by the hinges of hell, watching the inferno come straight to you.

The wind blasted us with heat, smoke so thick, boiling, blotting out the sun, the mountains, the sky — just something awful. Couldn't believe how fast those flames moved, how hot, how intense. Nobody had any idea what started the fire. Dry lightning perhaps. Good a guess as any.

The wind came from the west and northwest — almost always did — and just kept pushing that fire.

"Thank God you're here!" Tristram Gow sprinted toward us, pumping the major's hand, but the major turned away from Mr. Gow, and barked an order at us to get moving.

"What are we supposed to do?" Walter Butler asked.

I knew. Me and Tommy had seen fires in Texas, some worse than this one. We hobbled our horses, and walked toward the inferno, me emptying my canteen over a gunny sack, then tossing the canteen to the ground, and Tommy toting his rain slicker, not saying a word, not looking in my direction, just walking on. I pulled my bandanna over my mouth and nose, and just started pounding the flames, taking a place beside one of Mr. Gow's hands, armed with a broom. Must have been two dozen or more cowboys out there, swinging, swatting, sweating, but I didn't spot John Henry. Fighting right alongside us waddies were even a couple of grangers trying to make something out of their homesteads. Wasn't but a handful of farmers up here in those days, this being cattle country. And sheepherders. There were plenty of sheepmen, most of them north or west of the Bar DD and 7-3 Connected ranges.

This fire could have been wilder. Grass had been pretty much overgrazed. That helped a mite. Still, it turned brutal real quick.

We attacked those flames. Backing up to keep from getting burned alive. Couldn't hardly breathe.

Tell you the truth, I was still a heap mad at Tommy, so I hit those flames with that wet gunny sack like I was punching Tommy's nose out the back of his head. Pictured myself doing it. I thought the long ride would have calmed me down, but it didn't do nothing but give me a lot of hours to hurt and fume, especially since I'd been riding right behind that spring wagon that was carrying the womenfolk, including Lainie.

Might could have burned to death, mad as I was, if it hadn't been for Tommy.

There I stood, that gunny sack dried out by now, starting to smolder, and I felt someone pulling on my shoulder, soft at first, then almost jerking me off my feet. Eyes pained from the smoke, heat, dust, I whirled to find Tommy.

"Move!"

"Get away from me!" I barked at him. Went back to the fire, but Tommy grabbed me, turned me around, shoved me forward.

"What's the matter . . ." — he coughed, pointed — ". . . with you?"

That's when I realized that me and Tommy were the only ones still at the line. Everybody else had pulled back another two hundred yards or so.

"Move, Jim!" Tommy yelled. "Run!"

I was hacking something awful, but I staggered on ahead, past a burned-up broomstick that Mr. Gow's hired man must have dropped, felt Tommy behind me. We got back to our horses, where the major told us to mount up and ride for a hill. We'd make another stand there.

Which is what we did, and that's where I found John Henry Kenton. Never would have dreamed I'd ever see him like that, his hands gripping a Fire Fly — that's a single-wheeled hoe, cultivator, and plow, all in one — helping a sodbuster unload it from a wagon.

Mr. Gow kept yelling at Major MacDunn that plowing would save the grass on the other side.

"It will not work!" the major barked.

"It might," Mr. Gow pleaded.

"The winds are too strong, Tristram. The fire will leap across your break."

"Not if we make it wide enough."

"There's no time for that! Kenton!"

John Henry gladly took his hands off that plow.

"Your name is Kenton, right?"

John Henry's head bobbed.

"Get your saddle gun, Kenton, and follow me." Next, the major threw me a sheathed skinning knife. John Henry understood — can't say I did — and Mr. Gow ran to the plow that John Henry had just abandoned. Which was fine with Major MacDunn.

"You do it your way," the major said. "I need you, too, O'Hallahan. And you." He pointed at Ish. "Rest of you, plow your fields."

I've thought about it a lot over the years. I'd like to think the major was doing what had to be done. Maybe it was the major who saved the rest of that range, maybe it was Mr. Gow and the farm equipment some sodbusters had brought over. Maybe it was the both of them. I'd like to believe that the major wasn't . . . well . . . no point guessing. Like I said, I never could predict the major, nor figure out his motives. And he wasn't the only cattleman who fought a prairie fire that way.

John Henry knew what to do. He shot the first steer we rode up to, trying to run from the onrushing fire, and didn't stop, kept riding ahead till he had killed another. The major galloped over a hill, where his rifle boomed.

Didn't disgust me, skinning that dead steer. Wasn't like earlier that spring in Texas. I'd figured out what we were doing by then. Basically I just gutted that animal, split it in two, skinning one side. Wasn't like I was letting it bleed out before carving up steaks. About the time I was finished, John Henry rode up, and I helped him tie the end of his

119

lariat around the dead steer's carcass. "Get that other one I killed," he told me. Then he spurred that big sorrel and loped out, dragging the bloody steer over the flames, right on the edge of the fire. He rode about a hundred yards, turned the sorrel around, rode right back, pulling the steer over the flames.

Tommy followed the major over the hill to skin the beef he'd killed, and I chased after Ish to the other steer John Henry had shot dead. Skinned that one, too, sort of, and watched Ish drag its body. By then, the major was pulling the one he'd killed and Tommy had skinned.

The major, John Henry, and Ish rode in front of the flames, just a little ways, then turned around. Reason for that was to keep the horses' hoofs from getting charred. Tried to, anyway, although Ish Fishtorn had to kill the horse he was riding — its legs got so burned. That was the cost. Part of it.

I watched in awe for a moment, then, coughing, I hurried back to Mr. Gow. Had to help. Which is one of the good things I remember about my first year in Montana. You hear about how sodbusters and ranchers never got along, how sheepmen and cowboys hated each other, but in Montana, we all worked together, let each other alone.

There were no range wars, nothing like that. Not then. Wouldn't say we respected each other, but we let each other be. On that day, up along Muddy Creek, sodbusters, and ranchers, and sheepmen fought that fire, side-by-side.

Well, the cattle we'd killed, the break the others had dug — we stopped the fire, let the flames just burn themselves out, and, while Mr. Gow and his son rode around the blackened earth to see how bad things were, the major led the rest of us back to the Gow headquarters. The grangers packed up their plows, went back toward their homesteads. The sheepmen went back to their flocks. Nothing left at the 7-3 Connected but cowboys, faces so blackened, hair singed, so filthy they looked like something out of a bad dream.

Still coughing like a lunger, eyes red, face smeared with soot, I could hardly breathe, but Mrs. Gow made me drink some tea, and she just sat beside me, washing my face, bathing my eyes with a cool, damp towel, me too tuckered out to resist. Didn't like anybody fretting over me, nursing me, but I'd taken the worst of it. Nobody else got so much smoke in his lungs, but it was my fault. Hadn't been so riled at Tommy, I wouldn't have almost gotten myself burned like bacon. Good thing was that I wasn't mad at Tommy any more, even if I saw him sitting on the ground, eating his supper while talking sweetly to Lainie.

"I am so glad we didn't have to go into that root cellar," Mrs. Gow told me.

The ranch wasn't much to look at. Wondered what John Henry thought of it. I mean, Major MacDunn had a real house, but the Gow place wasn't nothing but a soddie, and the bunkhouse was a dugout. Pretty uninspiring, and the Gows had been in Montana a lot longer than the MacDunns. Except for Mrs. Gow. Melvina was her name.

"I hate the root cellar," she told me.

"How come?" I asked. It looked deep enough to keep a lot of food, probably a man like the major could even stand up inside it. Come in handy during a bad winter, and I warrant the major had been right. Even had the flames been higher, the wind a bit stronger, the grass taller, I imagine the major would have been right, and the women would have been spared had they taken refuge inside the root cellar.

"It's like a tomb," she said. She wasn't looking at me, just staring off at the smoky haze. The sinking sun was just a wild orange ball, soft, fuzzy. She shook and sighed.

"And the wind. . . ."

"It blows out here," I admitted.

"Do you ever get used to it?"

I shrugged, suddenly wanting to be with John Henry, even Tommy, even Mrs. Mac-Dunn.

She smiled at me, feeling better I guess, and asked how I was doing. "I'll be fine," I said, though my lungs still ached.

"I have only been here since March," she said. "Tristram did not want me to come until he felt the ranch was secure."

"I thought Mister Gow's been here for ten years."

"Eleven," she said. "Camdan and I did not make the journey till. . . ." Her face changed. She looked horrified, and I didn't know what to make out of it, till she asked: "Good heavens, child, what happened to your face?"

"Run into something in the bunkhouse," I mumbled.

Well, the ladies decided to fix us a celebration supper, and went to making baking-powder biscuits, beef stew. Mrs. Gow even went into the root cellar she hated so and come out with a bottle of Dewar's, which she passed around. Even let me and Tommy have a swig. Walter Butler wouldn't taste it, though. 'Course, John Henry took the biggest pull on that bottle.

Long past dark, Mr. Gow and his son rode up, while we was celebrating, bragging about all our heroics, telling some fine lies. Me and Tommy laughing aplenty, but that was like us two. Fought like brothers, 'cause we really were brothers, but seldom held a grudge. Mrs. Gow, who hadn't even sampled that Dewar's, was showing us some new dance popular over in Scotland, trying to get Ish Fishtorn to learn how to make those steps, and I swear the major slapped his thighs and laughed so hard his eyes teared. Till Mr. Gow rode right up to him.

Guess we had started that fandango way too early.

"You just had to do it," Mr. Gow said, his lips tight, face white underneath all that soot, all that rage.

"I saved your ranch, Gow," the major said.

"Tristram . . . ," Mrs. Gow began.

"Shut up, Melvina."

Camdan, on a buckskin right behind his father, looked paler than his father. His mother brought her hands to her mouth. I wanted to be as far away from that place as possible.

"Your firebreak would never have held,

Gow," the major said. "Not as dry as it has been."

"I do not fault your methods," Mr. Gow said. "But you. . . ." That was about as close as I ever come to hearing Mr. Gow cuss a man. I swear Mr. Gow started to cry. "Thousands of steers and heifers, but, you, you . . . you killed a magnificent, five-hundred-dollar Aberdeen Angus bull!"

CHAPTER TWELVE

Summer seemed to pass quickly after we rode back to the Bar DD, leaving Mr. Gow grieving over the loss of his prime bull, leaving Camdan Gow with his folks, and a lot of burned-up range.

I'd go to school, read some with Lainie, watch Lainie and Tommy hold hands. I'd work with Gray Boy and some other widow-making bronc's. I chopped wood. Gathered dried cow dung. Mended leather. Practiced my ciphers. Rode Crabtown. Listened to Ish Fishtorn's stories in the bunkhouse. Played some mumblety-peg with Walter Butler. So things went.

The better days of life were ours;
The worst can be but mine:
The sun that cheers, the storm that
*   lowers,*
Shall never more be thine.
The silence of that dreamless sleep

I envy now too much to weep;
Nor need I to repine
That all those charms have pass'd away,
I might have watch'd through long decay.

That's a poem by Lord Byron. Tommy often recited it when we'd be cowboying because the older hands loved to hear Tommy quote some fancy writings. So did Mrs. MacDunn. About a week after the big fire, she was having us all read poetry, and Tommy stood at the head of the class. He didn't need a book to read from, he knew Byron so well. So did I. Fact of the matter is that I was a bit riled at him for using that poem because I figured that I'd heard it enough that I would be able to recite it, and impress Mrs. MacDunn.

Just as Tommy had finished, as Mrs. MacDunn applauded like she was at an opera house, Camdan Gow walked into the schoolhouse. Didn't say much, and everybody except Walter Butler had brains enough not to ask him where he'd been all this time. Camdan didn't answer him, just walked to his desk, and sat down.

"We are so glad you are here, Camdan," Mrs. MacDunn said. She didn't ask him anything, either. I wondered, though. Studied on it more than I did my ABCs, because it didn't make sense to me why Camdan Gow would have come back to the Bar DD. His father thought the major had killed that pricey black bull on purpose. To spite him. Or for some reason that only the major and Mr. Gow knew. Camdan liked school no better than I did. No, sir. Didn't make any sense at all.

A few nights later, when Tommy and I were alone in the bunkhouse, I asked him about it.

Tommy snorted. "You've seen where he lives. Wouldn't you rather stay here than in that sod house? A broom made out of willow twigs? A pantry built of tomato can cases? It's not exactly homey there."

For a moment, I thought again of John Henry, wondered how he liked working for the 7-3 Connected, rough as it was. Then I considered Camdan.

"No, Camdan wouldn't run off," I told Tommy. "He loves his folks too much. They sent him back here."

"Maybe Mister Gow isn't mad at Major MacDunn any more."

"Seemed mad after the fire," I argued.

Tommy let out a long sigh. "It's the law," he finally replied, and I could tell my questions irritated him. "He has to attend school."

I shook my head. "That ain't it."

"What makes you say so?"

"Well, I figure we're too far away from Helena. The law don't care what's going on up on the Sun River or Muddy Creek."

The look of annoyance left Tommy's face. He had pulled a book by Mark Twain out of his war sack, and sat on his bunk. "If you figured that out," he said, "why are you still going to school? Why are you still here?"

"I been tempted to leave," I told him. "Especially early on. But I started thinking about what John Henry first told me and you when we started riding with him. You remember?"

His head shook slightly.

"He said he was pure fury on a tenderfoot who'd quit on him, but he'd be a real good teacher. . . ."

"Mentor," Tommy corrected, suddenly smiling. "He said *mentor*."

"Mentor. That's right. Said he'd be a real good mentor to even a tenderfoot who stayed."

Tommy's face brightened. "He said . . . 'I'll be proud to partner with a couple of stayers.'"

"That's right. And we told him we was . . . we *were* stayers. Not quitters. So I'm no quitter. I'm a stayer. Even if I don't really cotton to it all. Couldn't let John Henry down. Or you. I'm glad I didn't quit, too. Mostly glad anyway."

Laughing, he slapped my shoulder. "I'm glad you're here," he told me. "Come here. This is a good book. Maybe even better than *Treasure Island.* Let's practice your reading."

Oh, you bet I kept my eyes on Camdan, though. Spent more time sneaking peeks at him than I did at Lainie MacDunn. It wasn't like he kept doing things to cause any suspicion. He read a poem at school. Think it was something by Poe. Knew his math. Did his chores without complaint. Said — "Yes, ma'am." — to Mrs. MacDunn and — "Yes, sir." — to Ish, Gene Hardee, and the major. After a couple of days back at the Bar DD, he even started grinning when Walter Butler told one of his jokes.

But. . . .

Well, there was one time, afternoon, hot and windy like it had been all summer, dust blowing across the hills, and I come up to the big corral where we had penned Mr. MacDunn's two big Angus bulls. We'd been holding them at the ranch since me and John Henry and Tommy first brought them up, letting them fatten up before turning

130

them loose in the fall. Camdan was forking them some hay, and I had stepped out of the barn after oiling the saddles. I watched him for a moment, walked over to the corral. His back was to me, and, when I called out his name, he liked to jumped all the way to Utica.

"How much hay you planning on feeding them bulls?" I asked.

He stared at me, only for a while there it struck how he didn't really see me, recognize me. Know what I mean? Finally Camdan blinked, glanced around him, shook his head, and looked at me once more.

"Best get some of that hay back out here," I told him. "Major MacDunn don't like waste. Hay ain't cheap."

With a short nod, Camdan tossed the pitchfork over the top post, and started climbing the corral. The Angus bulls inside snorted, and, though I didn't like it much, I climbed up after him.

"I did not ask for your help," he said defiantly.

"Best hurry," I told him as I jumped down. "Those bulls ain't in the mood for any company."

After a quick look over his shoulder, he muttered a curse about those bulls, and started pitching forkfuls of hay over the fence, with me on the other side scooping up handfuls myself while keeping a close watch on those two Aberdeen Angus bulls.

Got out of there without any problems. The major never knew what had happened, and had I told Tommy or Lainie about it, they would have just explained it all away as Camdan Gow being addle-brained. As it was, I never told anyone what had happened, and, truthfully, it didn't amount to much. Didn't have to mean anything. Yet it festered at me.

'Course, had I been a real friend, I could have asked Camdan about it, asked him if anything was bothering him, asked him if I could help him somehow, asked to be his friend. But I didn't. After we were out of the corral, and he was raking up some of the loose hay, I just walked back to the bunkhouse. We never said anything more about it.

Never said anything about what happened two nights later, either.

He didn't wake me up. Wasn't really asleep, I think, like I had been waiting all night, all the past several days, really, for whatever was going to happen.

The floorboard squeaked. A long pause. The soft falling of footsteps. Ish Fishtorn's snores. Walter Butler muttered something in his sleep. Another few steps, and the moaning of the night wind as somebody opened the door. The door closed, and I heard nothing but snores.

Quickly I swung up, grabbing for my boots, debating whether I should wake Tommy. I didn't, and moved to the door in a crouch, waiting, listening. I went out the door quickly, closed it, knelt. I watched.

With the moonlight, it didn't take long for me to spot Camdan. Swallowing, I went after him, trailing, the wind cool, biting, and screaming like a fiend. Camdan might not have heard me had I been wearing spurs and beating a drum. Something glinted in the moonlight. It had to be a gun, and then I got really scared, could just picture him walking into the MacDunn's house and murdering the major, Mrs. MacDunn — and Lainie! I moved after him, running, but stopped when he walked right on past that house. What struck me next was that he was planned to take his own life with that revolver in his hand. I didn't know what to do. He went past the barn before stopping at the corral. No longer running, but just as scared, I walked slowly toward him, watched his right arm raise. It weaved uncontrollably, and he had to lift the left to steady the long-barreled revolver.

Unceremoniously chewing his cud, the nearest Aberdeen Angus bull looked up from the remnants of hay. Camdan Gow gasped, tried to steady the gun.

"Camdan?"

He whirled, let out a sharp cry, and now I looked down that long pistol barrel. Not for long, though. Made myself stare into Camdan's eyes. The gun weaved.

I wet my lips. "Is that why your father sent you back here?" I made myself talk. "To kill the major's two bulls?"

I wasn't sure he heard me over the wind.

"For revenge?" I asked.

The gun barrel spun like an out-of-control watch hand. Camdan tried to steady it.

Boy, don't you get to thinking that I was some brave hero. Camdan hadn't gotten around to cocking the single-action revolver, and, as wild as he kept shaking, I must have felt pretty confident he couldn't hit me if he took to shooting. He stood there, tears pouring down his face.

"You can't do it, Camdan," I said. "Major MacDunn didn't kill your pa's bull on purpose. He was just trying to save your grass. That's all. Bull was closer than any steers or heifers, and that fire kept coming fast. He saved your pa's ranch." Now, I was talking just to be talking. Not sure if I believed what I was telling Camdan, but a boy'll do funny things when he's staring down a gun barrel, even if the gun ain't cocked, and the gunman ain't Wild Bill Hickok. "Camdan, you can't kill those two bulls, no matter what your pa wants. It just ain't right. You know it. Besides, I don't think your pa really wants you to do this. Certainly not your ma."

The whirling gun slowed.

"Camdan," I tried again.

The gun fell to his side, and Camdan walked to me, dropped the big revolver at my feet, and whispered: "Papa had nothing to do with this." He went back to the bunkhouse.

I stood there, oblivious to the wind, for another two or three minutes before I picked up the pistol. Then I started trembling, shaking worse than Camdan had. Finally I somehow walked back to the bunkhouse, quietly slipped the revolver into my war bag, and laid down.

Didn't sleep none that night.

For another week or so, I couldn't think straight, do anything right. Camdan — it really surprised me that he stayed after he went out to kill those two bulls — remained the same: quiet, alone, doing his chores.

'Course, we kept away from each other.

"Let's get out of here," I told Tommy one Sunday evening when he was reading to Lainie and me. Just blurted it out.

"What are you talking about?" he asked, closing the book.

"I got a bad feeling about this place," I said.

"Jim!" Lainie cried. "I don't want you to leave."

"Yeah," Tommy said. "Remember what you told me about John Henry. . . ."

I cut him off right quick. "This ain't no place for us, Tommy! I got a bad. . . ."

"Quit being superstitious!"

"Please don't leave," Lainie said again, and Tommy give her a stern look.

I sighed. "I don't want to leave, either," I told her, and looked at Tommy. "But . . . I. . . ." I didn't know what else to say.

"Grow up, Jim Hawkins. You're either a stayer or a quitter," Tommy snapped. "Which is it?"

I didn't answer, but I knew I'd stay. Stay for Tommy. Maybe stay for Camdan Gow's sake. Maybe my own. Mostly for Lainie. I still had a bad feeling about the Bar DD, about Montana, but I was a lot like Camdan Gow. I'd just bottle it all up inside me, not talk to anyone about it. Bottle it up till I exploded.

Back in the bunkhouse, I made sure Walter Butler wasn't sticking his nose in my business, and grabbed my war bag. I withdrew the revolver Camdan had dropped by my feet, and stared at it. It was an old Army Colt, a relic from the War Between the States that had been modified to take brass cartridges, some flakes of rust on the barrel and cylinder. Not fancy, but serviceable. Scratched rudely into the walnut stock was a crooked letter *K*.

Often, John Henry Kenton had told me and Tommy that he'd give that pistol to the first one of us who became a man.

Chapter Thirteen

"Grandpa," the boy asks, "what happened to these trees?"

They had made it into Sun River Cañon, setting up camp a few miles back at the edge of the cañon near the remnants of what his grandfather calls a line camp, one washed away in a flood decades ago. Now they ride deeper into the cañon carved by the river, the water roiling from the early spring run-off, climbing into the forest, the giant blue sky partially hidden by cobweb-like clouds. Jim Hawkins has been stopping frequently, looking across the Sun, eyes searching, but seldom talking.

The flask of Dewar's is long empty, and, like it, Jim Hawkins's monologues have dried up. He has climbed back inside his shell, reticent, hard. He swings his horse around, and approaches Henry Lancaster, sees where the boy is pointing.

An ancient pine, bark long gone, sawed off

at a height of about four feet. Ages ago. The boy counts about a dozen similar dead trees, some even cut down at heights of up to six feet, while others have rotted and collapsed, being overtaken by new, fresh growth.

"Hackers," the grandfather answers, and spits.

"Hackers?"

"They were cutting down trees, even in the winter." He looks away.

"For firewood?"

"Railroad," he answers. "Let's ride up a little more."

It will be like this for the next couple of days, but Henry will be persistent, asking questions, getting answers, prodding a story out of Jim Hawkins. Every once in a while, however, his grandfather will open the spigot again, letting his story come out.

Autumn, 1886

It seems the grass is already cured and the only effect this rain will have upon it, if any, will be to reduce it in strength, washing out the qualities which render it so much more nourishing than ordinary hay or grass.

— *Yellowstone Journal and Live Stock Reporter,* October 16, 1886

Chapter Fourteen

Hackers used the road from Hannah Gulch all the way to Tie Camp Creek, twenty-four miles, hauling wood for the railroad they were building.

Me and Tommy come up here that fall of '86. Well, first we went to Helena. Me and Tommy, Ish, and Gene Hardee driving four wagons. And Major MacDunn. He just plucked us two kids out of school. Since I wasn't about to question the major, I asked Gene Hardee what we were doing, and he said we needed supplies. With the root cellar already full of potatoes and turnips, I told him four wagons was a lot of supplies, and he reckoned that was the truth. I told him they must be important supplies if the foreman *and* the major was fetching them, and he started brooding. Wouldn't say a word, but before I could pester Ish with questions, Tommy elbowed me in my side. I held my tongue, climbed into my wagon, followed the rest of them to Helena.

One afternoon on the trail down to Helena, I looked up, saw a flock of birds high in that clear Montana sky.

"Look at them ducks," I said.

Tommy, oh, that Tommy, he had to correct me, point out to the others just how ignorant I was.

"They're geese," he said.

I reckon they were at that. I could hear them honking, making a perfect V as they flew.

"Wish you had your Ten Gauge, Gene," Ish Haley said, flicking the reins. "Some greasy goose meat would sure hit the spot."

Major MacDunn, now he didn't care about any birds, just kept riding south, sitting deep in his saddle, his mind a thousand miles away, oblivious to the flock following him overhead, then passing him. On the other hand, Gene Hardee had reined in, took off his hat, and spied on those geese till they were out of sight.

"Funny," Gene said.

"How's that?" Ish asked him.

Gene Hardee put his hat back on, and shrugged. "Kind of early for geese."

Left the wagons at the depot, waited for the

major to talk to the fellow running the station there, then he came back, told us the train wasn't due for two more hours. The major said he'd stand us all to some dinner at the Bonanza State Restaurant before he had to get to a big meeting of the Montana Stock Growers Association at the Grandon Hotel.

Hadn't really paid much attention to the city when me and Tommy and John Henry first arrived that summer. Didn't remember much of it, except Teddy Roosevelt talking at the depot about barbed wire. Was different on this second trip. Never seen so many fancy people in all my days. That was Helena. Gold, and livestock, and banks, and real estate had made a lot of folks rich. Millionaires they were. I heard once that some fifty millionaires hung their hats in Helena. No wonder Major MacDunn and the other leading stockmen were meeting here.

You've seen the Grandon Hotel, I reckon, big, fancy hotel at Sixth and Warren. It was fancy then, too, although they hadn't yet added that third story or the cupola. That's where we found *Madame* Samson, The Gifted Prophetess. She wasn't no millionaire, but she drew a crowd in front of the hotel where the cattlemen were meeting. Drew more folks than even Teddy Roosevelt.

Never seen a woman dressed as fancy as she was, like she had stepped straight out of one of those stories about the Arabian nights. She had set up a table on the boardwalk, charging anyone interested in hearing his or her future a whole dollar. I didn't think the major would hold no truck with a soothsayer, but he stopped, and we watched her for a couple of minutes. She told a young woman with blonde hair that her baby would be a healthy boy, told a man in a checkered vest that he should not draw to an inside straight, and then Major MacDunn sat down, flipped her a dollar, and asked her about the coming weather. My jaw liked to have dropped to the pine planks at my feet.

She turned some cards — not poker cards, either — and looked up with eyes blacker than any I'd ever seen, and said in an accent that sounded mighty strange: "The loss in cattle this year will not be markedly large."

The major's face brightened. "*Madame* Samson," he said, tipping her another dollar, "if you have correctly called this tune, come back to Helena in the spring, and you shall do better business than Hennesy's saloon."

Some burly men loaded our four wagons at the depot, not a one of us saying a word as we watched. My mouth had turned to sand, and after the tarps were tied over our freight, after Gene Hardee had signed some papers, we climbed into the wagons, released the brakes, and headed out of Helena.

"What about Major MacDunn?" I asked.

"Major's got his meeting," Gene Hardee answered. "He'll be here another day or two. Don't want us hanging around town."

Nobody said anything else till we made camp that night, and even I had enough brains not to join the conversation.

"This isn't going to set well," Ish said.

"You ride for the brand," Gene Hardee reasoned. "MacDunn pays me money. I don't question his orders, nor his motives."

"I don't like it," Tommy said, and I tried to elbow him in the ribs, get him to shut up. Our cargo made him mad, too. I was like Gene Hardee, maybe. I rode for the brand, drew wages from the major, didn't want to question his orders, but I had seen enough of barbed wire — even though this was a different brand than Scutt's, something called Haish's patented Original S —

to last a lifetime. Devil's rope. John Henry had come more than a thousand miles to get away from that wire, and here it was. Being hauled by me and Tommy.

Tommy told them about the drift fence, how much havoc it had caused in the Panhandle, and Ish and Gene Hardee listened solemnly, but, when Tommy finished his story, Ish said: "This isn't Texas, Tommy. And Major MacDunn isn't building a drift fence."

"What would you know about it?" Tommy yelled, shooting to his feet. "You're nothing but a knock-kneed Oregonian son-. . . ."

Ish slapped him down with his hat before Tommy could finish, and, when Tommy jumped up, Ish knocked him down again. I started after Ish myself, but something caused me to change course, and I leaped in front of the cowhand and tackled Tommy, held him down, which took some doing, Tommy typically being not only smarter, but faster and stronger than me.

"Let me go!" Tommy yelled, but I squeezed him harder. Gene Hardee had also grabbed Ish's arms, pinned them back, but I could make out Ish's head nodding, his eyes not so angry.

"Let it go," I told Tommy. "That's Ish . . .

our friend.. . . . . You ain't . . . fighting . . . him."

Finally I loosened my grip. Gene Hardee made them two shake hands, be pals again, and things settled down.

It rained on the ride back. Not much of a rain, and, like God wanted to match our moods, He turned the rain into hail. We got beat by those hailstones, about the size of my thumbnail, a good ten, fifteen minutes. Long time for a hailstorm. It broke a bird's wing. I remember that. Saw the bird hopping along, flapping its one good wing, on the side of the road. We didn't stop, of course, to help it.

Tommy stayed. He was a stayer. But he wasn't the same Tommy O'Hallahan that I'd ridden with up the trail. I suspect he stayed because of Lainie MacDunn. Same as me.

CHAPTER FIFTEEN

See that tree, boy? The marks on it? Up higher. There you go. Grizzly sign. Marked his territory by slashing the trunk, letting everyone know he's *segundo* of this outfit. Bent it, too, likely from rubbing against it. You probably could have found some grizzly fur in the bark before winter came along. From the looks of that mark, he did that sometime last summer or thereabouts. He ain't around now. Horses would have caught his scent, but we might best head back to camp, just to be safe.

Reminds me of the time Tommy roped an old silvertip.

When we first started riding together, Tommy didn't know nothing about roping, but he had a stubborn streak in him, a determination, and, more important-like, he had John Henry for a teacher. Tommy beat himself black and blue trying to master a lariat, but he did it. Down in Texas, boys used to bet on him roping a coyote. So Tommy was the best roper, and me a pretty good bronc' buster. 'Course, John Henry was best at everything.

Well, after we got the wire hauled down from Helena, Major MacDunn let me and Tommy start working the fall gather. Oh, we still had school Mondays through Thursdays, but we didn't have to go to school — Mrs. MacDunn frowned on that — Fridays. I suspect that was a compromise between the major and the missus, him wanting us to earn our keep seven days a week. So on Thursday, after school, we'd mount our horses and ride over toward the Sawtooths, helping out Fridays and Saturdays and partly on Sundays — Mrs. MacDunn must have really stewed on that, what with us missing church and all — before coming back to the Bar DD headquarters that afternoon.

Must have happened the second weekend. Ish Fishtorn was bossing us, with Gene Hardee ramroding another group on the far side of Castle Reef, and he had me night hawking the remuda. Never cared for being a night hawk. Always figured that was a job for some tenderfoot, and I fancied myself more as a top hand. Yet I sure looked like a tenderfoot, and riled all the grown-ups in our outfit, because the horses scattered Friday night and Saturday night.

"Boy, can't you do nothin' right?" said Busted-Tooth Melvin. "We burn daylight chasin' down the mounts you scared off!"

I promised it wouldn't happen again, and Ish took me aside, told me it better not happen again, said if it did, I'd be back in school and church, and they'd let Walter Butler night hawk. So Saturday night, with it raining slight but steady, I aimed to keep them horses in one bunch. Around midnight, the rain turned to sleet, but I rode around the herd, singing softly with my teeth clattering, doing my job, making sure I stayed awake by chewing tobacco and rubbing the juice in my eyes. Burned like blazes, but I told myself that at least my eyes were warm. The sleet stopped an hour or so later, and the horses seemed settled down, and I started to feel a little better. Cold, but relaxed.

Right before dawn, they all busted loose.

Well, you never seen such a ruction. The horses didn't just scatter, they stampeded. Some of them ran right through camp, and I'd stupidly thrown my saddle on Gray Boy that night, and he took to bucking, had me pulling leather, hanging on for dear life. Most of the boys had their best horses handy, but it took some doing for them to get a foot in the stirrup. Couldn't hear a thing but horses snorting and men cussing, and most of those cuss words were aimed at me.

Gray Boy pitched me into a clump of brush, but I rolled over, and went running after him. It was light enough to see, and, when I saw what had rattled those horses so, I slid to a stop.

Ish Fishtorn reined up, glaring at me. "Boy, you beat the Dutch! I bragged on you, said you had the makings, but. . . ."

When I pointed, he shut up. Me? I couldn't find the words, but Ish found them. He let out a whopper of a cuss.

About a dozen horses disappeared over a hill, chased by the biggest grizzly we'd ever seen. Would have been funny, if it wasn't our horses, and if I hadn't been afoot.

A whoop and a holler echoed across the still, cold morning, and Tommy whipped by us on Midnight Beauty at a high lope, working a loop over his head.

"That boy's crazy!" Once again Ish Fishtorn had found the words, but Tommy wasn't the only loco waddie in our outfit. Busted-Tooth Melvin galloped right behind him. Two other boys took up the chase, as well. Ish spurred his mount back to camp, and I resumed chasing after Gray Boy, who had the good sense to run in the opposite direction of the grizzly. Lucky for me, Gray Boy had settled down, and I only had to sprint a quarter mile or so before I caught up with him. He showed his temper a bit when I swung back in the saddle, but he was too tuckered out to put up much of a fight, and I spurred him after Tommy and the grizzly.

You know what they say about a bear? The smaller the ears, the bigger the bear. Well, that was one mighty big bear, looked more like a buffalo with that hump of muscle atop his shoulders, and its brown fur matted and shaggy. Fierce teeth and giant claws. Stood close to eight feet tall on its hind legs.

Wish I could have seen it when Tommy threw a perfect loop around the bear's left forepaw. Tommy and Melvin caught up to him first, in a coulée, and the griz' turned its attention on the cowboys. Midnight Beauty wasn't so co-operative, but Tommy got a dally around his horn, leaned hard on the far stirrup, while Melvin's second try caught the bear's head. Only problem was Melvin got too close, and, when that grizzly roared, Melvin's bay threw him toward the moon. Horse went running after the rest of the remuda, and Melvin grabbed his rope, screaming for help, pulling in the slack, bracing the lariat against his back, backing to the edge of the coulée. Tommy couldn't hold that bear much longer, but Paul Scott, a black-mustached man on a zebra dun, got his lariat around one of the bear's back legs, and Old Man Woodruff done the same.

That's about the time I rode up, but my lariat had been knocked off somewhere during Gray Boy's bucking spell, and I don't reckon Gray Boy would have let me get any closer to that grizzly than the top of the coulée.

Grizzly kept roaring, horses kept dancing, Melvin kept grunting, and Tommy kept laughing. Ain't a one of us had a gun, and only Old Man Woodruff had a weapon of any kind, but I don't think his Barlow knife would do much good on a giant, ornery silvertip.

"Where's Ish?" Paul Scott yelled.

Looking over my shoulder, I spied Ish riding hard for us.

"I'll get him!" I yelled. Tell you the truth, it made me happy to get out of there. Well, I made a beeline for Ish, and told him what had happened. He pulled his horse to a stop, suddenly grinning up the biggest scheme I'd ever heard. I galloped back to the coulée.

"I found Ish," I told my pards. "Told him what you-all done."

"Where is he, damn it? What did he say?" Old Man Woodruff yelled above the grizzly's roars.

I grinned. "Said to tell you boys you best not let go of them ropes." Then, howling with laughter, I spurred Gray Boy back toward Ish, who sat doubled over in his saddle, cackling like a crazy hen.

Best laugh we'd had in a 'coon's age.

I asked Tommy why he done it, but he never answered nothing more than a shrug. Sport it was. Something new. 'Course, we killed the griz'. Ish had gone back to camp to fetch his Winchester, a big old Centennial model that sounded like a Howitzer, and we didn't leave the boys alone with their ropes for too long. Killed the bear, and had bear stew, and that thick hide of his made a great rug at the line shack over at Sun River Cañon.

Nobody had ever seen a bear that big, or one that hungry, and its coat seemed so heavy. We talked about that for a long time, and you should have seen the look on Lainie's face when we told that story once we got back to the ranch. Didn't have to stretch the truth any, either. A crazy thing to do.

Everybody said so. Everybody laughed. Except John Henry.

When John Henry surprised us with a visit one evening that week, Tommy couldn't wait to tell him about roping the bear, but John Henry had no interest in tomfoolery.

"Didn't expect to see MacDunn's two bulls," he said, and my stomach started acting funny. We were in the bunkhouse, and, when John Henry asked that question, Camdan Gow got up and left. Walter Butler followed, leaving us alone with John Henry.

"Major MacDunn hasn't turned them loose yet," Tommy said.

"I see."

I saw, too. With a heavy heart, I went over to my bunk, pulled that big Colt out of my war bag, handed it to John Henry, butt forward.

He let out a little snort. "The Gow kid didn't have it in him, eh?" Reaching for the gun, he looked at me, and asked: "What about you, Jim?"

When I couldn't find the words, he snatched the gun so hard, it like to have tore off my hand.

"Why do you think MacDunn killed Gow's bull?" he snapped.

"Put out that grass fire," I answered.

John Henry muttered an oath. "Don't be blind."

I smelled the whiskey on his breath.

"What's in those wagons?" he asked.

Lucky, canvas tarps still covered those reels of barbed wire, barrels of staples, and tools. They'd been sitting in the wagon for a couple of weeks, waiting for fence posts to get cut.

My throat felt parched. Tommy answered softly: "Supplies."

John Henry turned, stared at Tommy till he looked away, and then our old pard let out a heavy sigh. "You two are nothing but a couple of kiddoes," he said. "Green peas still. Hoped you might have earned this." He hefted the Colt, before shoving it in his waistband. "But I reckon not. You ain't men yet."

"Takes a big man to ask a kid like Camdan to shoot two helpless bulls," I said, and John Henry struck like a cat, pinned me against the wall, pressed his forearm against my throat. I thought he might kill me, but just as quick he let me go, took a deep breath, gathered my hat he'd knocked off, and dusted it on his chaps, then handed it back to me.

He almost apologized, but John Henry could never bring himself to say he was sorry. I didn't expect it from him, and I figured I was to blame for riling him so. Mean thing I'd said to my mentor.

"You best know one thing," John Henry said in a hoarse whisper. "Both of you. Tristram Gow needs some winter range. There's a fight coming, between Gow and Mac-Dunn. Part of it's over grass. Most of it's over MacDunn's wife."

"That's a. . . ." Yet Tommy couldn't finish, couldn't call John Henry Kenton a liar. Or maybe he didn't want his windpipe just about crushed by John Henry's arm.

"That's a what?"

"Nothing."

John Henry looked at Tommy. "You know what I'm saying is true, don't you, O'Hallahan?"

Tommy stared at his boots.

"Listen, boys." John Henry grabbed my shoulder, pulled me to his side, put his arm around me. "I didn't ride over here to start a fight. I was repping the Seven-Three Connected at the gather east of here, thought I'd pay you a visit. We're pards. You just need to know that when this fight comes, you boys need to be alongside me. On the right side. Gow's been here the longest. MacDunn's nothing but a foreigner. He don't even own this ranch. Bunch of Englishmen own it."

"Scots," Tommy whispered. "They're all Scots. Even the Gows."

"Makes no difference. You boys can help me out, though."

Wanted to say: *The same way you asked Camdan Gow to help you?* But I couldn't, didn't want to believe it was true. Besides, had I said it, John Henry would have strangled me.

John Henry didn't have a chance to say anything else. Lainie MacDunn walked into the bunkhouse, then, holding *Treasure Island* in her hand, startled to find John Henry here.

She looked away from John Henry, first to Tommy, then to me. John Henry's eyes followed hers.

"Mother would be glad to have you join us for supper," she said, but her voice was forced. "I'll tell her. . . ."

"No need, Miss MacDunn. Just rode over to see how the boys are doing." His eyes gleamed. "What brings you to a bunkhouse, ma'am? I mean . . . who'd you come to see, Tommy or Jim?"

She started to stutter, and I felt my ears turn red hot.

"I'd best ride, Miss MacDunn. Just paying a social visit. Tell your ma that Mister

Gow sends his regards. Be seeing you, pards."

Things were changing that fall. When we first came to the Bar DD, they told us that Mrs. MacDunn closed her school in mid-November. For us boys, just a few days after John Henry's visit, school stopped in October. Once again, the major stepped into the school, pulled every boy out who stayed at the bunkhouse. Mrs. MacDunn started to argue with him, saying that education came first, but this time she couldn't make him back down. We took the wagons loaded down with barbed wire.

First post hole we dug was at the base of Castle Reef. Fencing in the pasture. Saving grass, Ish explained. Didn't appear to be much to save, I thought, dry as it had been, but I didn't argue with him. Protecting the major's interest. Saving our future. *In the course of time,* Mr. Roosevelt had said. Major MacDunn had decided the time was now.

CHAPTER SIXTEEN

Oh, my God! Oh, my God! Oh, my God!

Huh . . . ? What? Where am . . . ? Oh. . . . It's all right, boy. I'm all right. Just a bad dream is all. *Whew.* Haven't had a dream like that in some twenty-five years. Don't matter what it was about. Just a nightmare. Put some wood on them coals, boy. Looks to be just a couple hours till dawn anyhow. Ain't going to go back to sleep tonight, that's certain sure.

Funny. Now I remember what happened clearly.

Stringing Jacob Haish's patented wire. Reels of devil's rope. Digging holes, pounding posts, and setting them eight to ten feet apart. Make that wire taut, Gene Hardee ordered us.

Ain't no job fitting for a cowboy to do, but we done it.

Me and Camdan Gow did most of the wire work, while Tommy and Walter Butler set the fence posts. We had a lever and a wire grab — the major had ordered some Sampson wire stretchers, but us kids didn't get to use those; they was confiscated by the grown-ups stringing wire on the other side of Castle Reef. While I stretched the wire, pulling that thing tight, Camdan nailed staples with his hammer, securing the wire to the post. Had to be sturdy, strong, braced for Angus or longhorn. Then we wrapped the wire around the corner post, nailing fence staples to hold it, pulled it to the next post, working from the top down. Tight. Tight. Tighter.

The staples we carried in cut-off boot tops, the bottoms sewed up, that we hung from our saddles. That way I told myself that we was at least working with horses. Better than what Tommy and Walter Butler was doing.

They worked from a wagon, which carried our barrels of staples, cedar posts, tools, and reels of wire. Mean-looking fence it was, too. Barbed wire had to hurt to do any good, the major said, and Original S would sure do that job. Probably even tear up hides, I thought, with terrible barbs just under two inches long, but the major said stubborn cattle had to learn things the hard way.

Wire had to hurt. . . .

Well, the posts was sharpened, pointed at one end. Like spears. So Walter and Tommy would swing a pick, dig some with these post-hole diggers, or crowbars, shovels. Get the post started. Then Tommy would climb back on the wagon, and start swinging a sixteen-pound cast-iron post maul, just start hammering that fence post deep into that hard ground. He'd have to sink a post two or three feet deep.

They was working ahead of us, a pretty far piece, and we'd come behind, stringing wire. Every so often, they'd drop another couple of reels of wire for us, then move on down with the wagon eight to ten feet, hammer in another post. You ever swung a sixteen-pound maul, boy? Work up a sweat, you will. Get to where your muscles scream in pain. But, being headstrong, Tommy wouldn't let nobody else do it. I volunteered often enough, but he said he didn't want to touch no barbed wire. Sounded like John Henry when he said it.

That's what we was doing.

It wasn't Walter Butler's fault. He was green at this kind of thing. Wasn't nobody's fault. Just an accident. I didn't see it. Busy stretching wire and holding it so Camdan could secure it to the post we was on.

Way down the fence line, Tommy dropped two reels of wire to the ground, and he and Walter started a post. Then Tommy climbed back on top of the wagon bed, lifted that maul, Walter holding the post steady. Problem is, Walter plumb forgot to set the brake on the wagon, and when Tommy swung that maul, and it hit the top of the post, the mules jumped. Can't explain it. We'd been at it all day, all week, and those mules had been hearing that sound all that time. Wouldn't figure them to be so skittish. Maybe something else frightened them. Don't rightly know for certain. But the wagon lurched, just a few feet, before the mules stopped, and Tommy, exhausted, off balance from swinging the heavy maul, fell. He flung the maul away, didn't want it to come down on him, and fell hard. Fell right on the open spool of barbed wire.

Then I heard the worst screams I ever heard.

Me and Camdan come running, found Tommy writhing on the ground, yelling. The blood. Blood just gushing.

"My eye!" he yelled. "I can't see!"

Walter just stood there, mouth open, frozen in some kind of panic.

Tommy's face had hit the reel of wire. I

guess he'd pushed himself up, turning his head, ripping his ear, then fell again, using his hands to break his fall, tearing gashes in both palms.

I pried his hands off his face, pressed my own to stanch the blood.

"Oh, my God! Oh, my God! Oh, my God! Oh, my God!"

His face was a mess. Might have cracked his cheek bone from hitting so hard.

Walter started — "I didn't mean. . . ." — before he collapsed on his knees, retching.

"Oh, my God! Oh, my God! Oh, my God! Oh, my God!"

Strange. Here's the thing. All these years, all the times I've remembered — never wanted to, mind you, but couldn't forget — that incident, pieced it together. All the times, I thought it was Tommy yelling: "Oh, my God." But now I recollect. Now I hear that voice.

It was me.

I turned, saw Camdan, face whiter than a sun-bleached bone.

"Camdan!" I barked. "Fetch Gene Hardee or Ish." Both had gone to the other side of Castle Reef, directing the fencing operation there. "Tell him what happened. Tell him we need help! Now! Now! You got to go now!"

Next I ordered Walter to loosen his bandanna, hand it to me.

When he did, I wadded it up, pressed it against the worst cuts. Used my own bandanna to wrap around Tommy's head. Hoofs sounded. That was Camdan riding off. I looked down that unfinished fence line, looked up at Castle Reef, and over at the Sawtooths. Never felt so far away, so hopeless.

"Walter, I need you to help me," I said. Surprisingly calm. Then to Tommy: "Tommy, we're going to get you to the line shack. You'll be all right."

"How bad is it?" he cried. "I can't see."

Ripped off my left shirt sleeve, used it to wrap his cut hands.

"You got blood in your eyes," I told him. "That's all. You're no worser than I was when I stepped on that cactus in Texas."

It was, of course, a lie.

His left eye was gone, and that wire had laid him to the cheek bone, mangled his ear, both hands. Bad hurt, he was, but Tommy was alive.

Problem was, he didn't want to be.

Nearest doctor was in Helena or Great Falls, so they were no help. Ish Fishtorn stitched Tommy up with horsehair, after we'd shaved his hair around the cuts, me and Gene Hardee holding Tommy down. None of us had any John Barleycorn to dull the pain. Nothing we could do for the eye. Once we got him stitched, patched up as best as we could do in a line camp, we unloaded one of the wagons of barbed wire, and hauled Tommy in the back all the way to the Bar DD headquarters. Then, it was Lainie and Mrs. MacDunn who were crying so terribly, Lainie most of all.

Tommy wouldn't see her. Rather, he didn't want her to see him.

"I'm a monster," he told me. "A hideous monster. Cyclops."

"No, you ain't," I said.

He told me to go to hell.

Went like that for a week, Tommy brooding, Lainie crying. Infection set in, and Major MacDunn had to cut off the remnants of Tommy's right ear. It's a miracle the rest of his wounds didn't bring him down with gangrene.

The first snow fell a week after the major had removed Tommy's ear. That's when I first noticed how peculiar Gray Boy looked. I was staring at him, when Major MacDunn came up to me, angry and mean. He whirled me around, demanded to know why I hadn't fed his two Aberdeen Angus bulls. I told him I had. He cussed me for a liar, grabbed my collar, dragged me all the way to the bulls' corral. Pressed me against the rails, then let go. I guess he could see the remnants of the hay I'd forked over.

"They have eaten it," he whispered. "All of it."

Never seen those bulls that hungry, and maybe he started to notice the same thing about those Angus as I had just noticed about Gray Boy.

Winter coats were coming on, earlier than usual, heavier. Something else struck me, and that was how silent the ranch had become. No birds. Least not so many of them. Even the ones that stayed north all winter had turned south.

"Jim?"

I jumped off the chair, spilling my coffee, and ran to Tommy's bunk. He sat propped up against the wall, his head still wrapped up like a mummy, face below the bandages pale, his one good eye red-rimmed.

"Yeah, Tommy."

"I want you to do me a favor."

"Anything. You want me to fetch you a

book to read?"

"I want you to write a letter."

I didn't know how to answer.

"Tell John Henry what happened."

He held up his bandaged hands. "I can't very well write with these."

"But John Henry can't read."

"Someone will read it to him. Tell him everything."

"Lainie," I tried, "would write a whole lot better than me. I could ask. . . ."

"NO!"

I gave it to Mrs. MacDunn, because I didn't know how one went about posting a letter, especially at the Bar DD. Smiling sweet but sad, she said she'd take care of it. I told her I'd pay whatever it cost, and she just nodded, and I left her.

Started back for the bunkhouse, but Lainie stopped me.

"How is Tommy?" she asked.

"He's mending. Some."

"Why doesn't he let me help him?" Her lips started trembling. I wanted to be long gone before she started bawling.

"You got to give Tommy some time, Lainie. He's prideful. Shames him to be hurt and. . . ."

"It's my father's fault! He and. . . ."

"It ain't nobody's fault. Just an accident. Could have happened to any one of us."

"But . . . it . . . happened to Tommy. . . ."

She started sobbing something awful. I couldn't leave her like that, so I come up to her, pulled her to me. Let her cry on my shoulder, all the while telling her that Tommy would be fine.

That was another lie.

Chapter Seventeen

Shortly thereafter, Major MacDunn sent me back to string wire at Castle Reef. Oh, he had learned from his mistake, wasn't about to let a bunch of boys do that work by themselves, so he made sure a grown-up supervised us. Sure, I hated leaving Tommy behind at the bunkhouse, but there just wasn't anything else I could do for Tommy. He had to mend himself. Thought about him, though, with every mile of wire I stapled to a post. Thought of John Henry, too. Thought of Judas.

Felt like Judas.

Bitterroot Abbott bossed us. Hadn't met him before, and the thing I noticed about Abbott was the fact that he didn't do no work, just watched. Slim fellow, he was, with bright blue eyes, rode a high-stepping dun horse, and kept a Winchester carbine across his lap. Bald on the top of his head, with hair that once looked to be blond before turning gray. Kept to himself mostly, cleaning a Smith & Wesson revolver, smoking his Bull Durham, and sipping from a flask till he'd emptied it. Had no use for a bunch of teenagers.

"Never does a lick of work," I complained to Walter Butler one night when Bitterroot went off to answer Nature's call. "Gene Hardee and Ish Fishtorn, now those boys'll work right alongside us. They don't fancy it. I mean, stringing wire ain't a fit job for a cowboy, but Gene and Ish, they do their share of the work. But not that bald-headed gent."

"He works," Walter said softly.

"I ain't seen it," I said.

Walter snorted, and sat up. "He rode with Major MacDunn with the Montana Stranglers," he said. "If I were you, I wouldn't get cross of Bitterroot Abbott. He's killed fifteen men."

"You mean he's a gunman? Like Wild Bill?"

"No," Walter said. Sounded kind of old for his age, like he knew a lot more than I did about those kinds of things. "He's nothing like Bill Hickok was."

"Well, what's he doing here for?"

"Working." Walter Butler threw his blanket over him, and rolled over.

Working? My stomach got all twisted. Major MacDunn had hired himself a gunman.

Tommy rode up one afternoon, must have been the last of October, maybe early November. Cold, it was. I remember Bitterroot Abbott laughing at my blanket. Thin, old woolly piece of moth holes that had served me well most nights down in Texas. "That hen skin won't protect you from *Kissin-ey-oo-way'-o.*"

I asked him: "Protect me from what?"

"Kissin-ey-oo-way'-o. It's Cree. Lived with them up north for three years when I was a young buck. *Kissin-ey-oo-way'-o."*

"What's it mean?" I asked.

"Well, you can't really put it in English. More like you have to feel it, and I've felt it. It means, more or less, that the wind blows cold. You'll feel it, boy, especially if that's all you have for your sougans."

"I feel it already," I told him.

"Hawkins," he said with a wry chuckle, "it ain't even cold yet."

That was the most I'd ever talked to Bitterroot Abbott. He sounded almost human then, made me forget that he was nothing more than a man-killer, but I pretty much forgot about our little talk because Walter

Butler ran to the campfire screaming that Tommy was coming, Tommy was coming. Sure enough, he was.

Wearing a new heavy coat with the sheepskin collar pulled up high, and his hat down low, Tommy swung down off Midnight Beauty. He looked a mess, but it did my heart a world of wonder to see him again. Tossed down his war bag, then untied a package he had secured behind his cantle, and threw it to me.

"Present," he said, "from Blaire Mac-Dunn. And Lainie."

The bandages were gone, and he had a big black leather patch over his missing eye. He wore a yellow silk bandanna kind of like a pirate. At least it reminded me of how I pictured some of Long John Silver's black-hearts from *Treasure Island.* It was wrapped around his head, like a lady's bonnet, hiding the missing ear, though he couldn't hide the scars, bruises, and scabs below his missing eye.

Still, he was Tommy, my pard. Only I couldn't think of anything to say to him.

"What brings you here?" Walter Butler asked.

"I earn my keep," he said, looking past our camp at the line of wire fence we'd already put up.

■ ■ ■ ■

What was the package? Oh, just a coat. Not a Mackinaw, and nothing as fancy as Tommy's sheepskin rig. A heavy canvas coat with a wool blanket lining. Nice to know the MacDunns thought of me. I thought about how cheap Mr. Gow was, figured he would have bought me a coat, too, but take it out of my wages.

When we started work next morning, I was pretty much all thumbs. Nerves took hold of Walter Butler, too. We just couldn't help it, what with Tommy back with us, just a few miles from where the terrible accident had happened. Tommy, he noticed it right off, turned angrily from a post he was setting, and just glared at us.

Didn't say a word, just stared with that blazing eye of his. Stared us down. I mumbled something to Walter, and started pulling wire from the reel.

Got to do some exploring, which suited me a sight better than building a barbed wire fence. I rode up into the mountains once, I recollect, picking up wood to use for our fires.

One time, me and Walter Butler come to a creek to find a muskrat, busy working on his house. Peculiar-looking animal, but he made me smile, watching him work, till he must have heard us or caught our scent, and disappeared in the woods.

"Big house he's building," Walter said. "Twice as big as anything I've seen."

"Maybe his gal's expecting triplets. Maybe he's been a mighty busy muskrat," I said, mighty pleased when Walter Butler blushed.

I've told you about Tie Camp Creek, where the hackers set up camp, cutting down wood for the railroad. We rode up to that camp one day to fetch some more fence posts, or at least prod the hackers into bringing us the supply they owed us.

"I bet they have some whiskey at that camp," Bitterroot Abbott said enviously.

"You should go," Tommy told him.

"Can't." He jutted his jaw at the wire. "Somebody's got to keep an eye on things, and I'm paid to do that."

"I'll stay," Tommy said.

"You?" Bitterroot had to choke back his laughter.

"I got one eye," Tommy snapped, "so I can keep an eye on things. And you'd be better at persuading those lumberjacks to fulfill their end of the bargain. You've said so yourself . . . Major MacDunn paid them for two loads of fence posts. We've gotten only one."

Bitterroot chewed on that thought with his salt pork, but finally shook his head. "Should wait. Hardee or Fishtorn should be here in a day or two. Send them up there."

"Suit yourself," Tommy said.

"We might be out of posts by tomorrow," Walter Butler said. I knew Butler's intentions. He was sick of working with wire, and probably still felt uncomfortable working alongside Tommy. He wanted to get out of camp.

Nobody said anything else for a spell, till I got up to throw another piece of wood on the fire.

"All right," Bitterroot said. "We'll ride up there come first light. You two boys will ride with me. Might need you to drive the wagons down."

I guess I knew what made Bitterroot decide to go, too. He had a big thirst for whiskey. Figured why Tommy volunteered to stay, too. Since the bad accident, he kept to himself.

Up higher, that's some country, but I tell

you what. That high up, it was a lot colder than it was down on the river. Those log men had also built themselves a couple of cabins, so I figured they planned to be up there in winter, too. They reminded me of the beaver pond we'd passed on the ride to Tie Camp Creek. Those lumber men were working hard, even harder than the beavers that had been stacking up piles and piles of saplings. 'Course, them beavers didn't have all the axes and adzes and saws and contraptions that we found at that camp of hackers.

We unsaddled our horses, rubbed them down, gave them some water and grain, and went to find the boss of the outfit, find out where our fence posts were, and why we hadn't gotten them yet. Never heard such noise, the flying sawdust worse than dust on a cattle drive. Saws singing, axes thudding, it wasn't nothing like a cow camp. Except for the men cussing.

They also had this monster-looking machine, which looked and sounded like a steamboat that was about to blow its boiler, belching out steam and cinders, shaking on its sled made of logs.

"What's that thing?" I yelled above the racket to a choker setter — that's what he called himself — a kid about my age, holding one end of a slack cable, with the other end attached to the drum on that noisy, steam-driven contraption.

He looked over my shoulder, and yelled back: "Steam donkey!"

Well, we watched him do his work, fasten that cable to a felled pine, watched that steam donkey start pulling the log, and then the kid warned us to get out of the way, and he took us to the boss' cabin.

"Best wait here, out of the way," he told us. "It's warmer inside, anyway."

The boss hacker was a thin, mustached Irishman named Burke. He poured us all two fingers of whiskey from a jug, pushed back his bowler, and give himself a whole tumbler full of rotgut.

"I work for Major MacDunn," Bitterroot told him. He killed his own drink, then took Walter's.

"I know."

"Then you know you owe the major another delivery of fence posts."

Burke sighed. "There will be no more fence posts, I'm afraid."

"Why's that?"

"We work for the railroad."

"You were working for the railroad when the major and you cut this deal."

"Aye. But that was before Mister Pego,

178

me boss, learned of that, *ahem,* side bet."
He drank thirstily, coughed, and wiped his
mouth with the back of his arm. "I'm lucky
to still have me job and me hide. It cost me
a month's pay."

Muttering an oath, Bitterroot refilled his
glass from the jug. He could have taken my
whiskey, like he'd done Walter's, because I
wasn't about to pour that stuff down my
throat.

"MacDunn'll have to find his fence posts
somewhere else. And since he hasn't paid
me for that second load, we're square."

Well, I didn't like that no better than Bitterroot Abbott, because I figured the major
would have me cutting down posts, and my
hands were blistered already.

"If you blokes will excuse me, I've work
to do." He reached for the jug, but Bitterroot put his hand on it, and gave him a hard
look. Burke swallowed, then turned, and
headed for the door. He stopped when
something made me ask him a question.

"How did your boss find out what you was
doing?"

"Someone wrote him. I do not know
who."

I had a pretty fair inkling, but I didn't say
so. Reckon if Tommy's hands had healed
enough to work fence, he could write a let-

179

ter to the Northern Pacific.

Waited till noon the next day, when Bitter-root's hangover allowed him to saddle his horse. We rode back to camp, empty-handed, me glad to get out of those mountains, away from those woodcutters, all that sawdust, and that screaming steam donkey.
Rode to our camp, and stopped, staring.

CHAPTER EIGHTEEN

"That double-crossing, little. . . ." Bitterroot Abbott swung off his horse, and walked to the fence line.

What was left of the fence line.

Tommy had poured coal oil over the remaining posts, and we found nothing left but smoldering ash and charred stumps. Sections of wire had been roped, and pulled down. Not all of it, mind you. Likely didn't have time or inclination to tear down that much fence. There was still a solid line from the base of the mountain to near the line shack, and other sections had been left alone. But what remained wouldn't keep cattle in.

Or out.

The wagon hauling the barbed wire was gone, but Bitterroot picked up the trail. It climbed into Sun River Cañon.

"You come with me," the gunman ordered me, and told Walter to raise dust, get to

Gene Hardee's camp on the far side of
Castle Reef, tell him what happened here.

"He had help." Bitterroot's voice sounded
harder, louder within the cañon walls.

We rode on, side-by-side. I didn't look
over at him.

"You hear what I said?"

"I heard you."

I wasn't that green. Now I never amounted
to much of a tracker, but I could tell from
the signs that at least two riders had destroyed much of our barbed wire fences,
and another man was leading a horse —
Midnight Beauty — while Tommy drove the
wagon up the trail alongside the river,
climbing higher into the mountains. Besides,
Tommy and his pard had left a calling card
at the line shack, the letter I'd written for
Tommy to John Henry, stabbed with a
butcher's knife in the front door. I'd found
it, took it down, and tossed it in the fire.

Bitterroot spit. "Did you know what he
was planning?"

"No."

I hadn't knowed. Didn't expect it, but
maybe I should have.

"You know who helped him, don't you?"

The tracks led off the road, through a clearing to the cliff's edge. Tommy and John Henry were long gone, but the mules grazed nearby. I dismounted, handed my reins to Bitterroot, walked to the drop-off. Peering over the side, I found the wreckage of the wagon, reels of barbed wire and barrels of staples smashed against the boulders some two hundred and fifty feet below.

The wind blew cold.

Kissin-ey-oo-way'-o.

I might have said it out loud. I know I thought it. The wind felt bitter, hard, even with me dressed in that new heavy coat the MacDunns had bought for me. The wind blew cold. But that wasn't really why I stood there, shivering.

"The war ain't just coming, boy," Bitterroot told me as we rode back down the trail, pulling the mules behind us. "It's started. Your pard just fired the first shot."

I didn't think so. The way I saw it, Major MacDunn pulled the trigger when he ordered miles and miles of Haish's barbed wire. Maybe he started it when he killed Mr. Gow's prize bull during the grassfire. 'Course, I knew better than to tell Bitterroot Abbott any of what went through my mind.

"It's going to be a bloody winter. So you

need to decide before we get back to the ranch who you plan on siding with." He reached over and grabbed my rein, stopping, staring at me.

"I'd hate to have to kill you, boy. Never wasted a bullet on a kid your age, but I will, if it comes to that."

Without saying a word, I looked at him, waiting for him to release my rein, which he did, with a heavy sigh.

"I don't blame your friend much," Bitterroot said. "Tommy did what I would have done, likely, had my face been beaten all to hell. And I don't blame Gow, either. He's just fighting to survive. Mostly, though, I don't blame Major MacDunn. He's got good reasons."

We'd reached the end of the cañon before he spoke again, following the rolling hills now, Castle Reef looming over our shoulders.

"Had me a wife once." Bitterroot's words surprised me, and I looked over at him. He kept staring straight ahead, talking. It's funny sometimes. Folks you hardly know will tell you something deep in their gut. Guess it can be easier to tell a complete stranger something like that than it would be to tell your closest friend or loved one. I don't know why. It ain't the same with me, I guess. I never told anybody nothing, hardly, except Lainie. Told her everything. Most everything. And now, I'm telling you. Even what I never told your grandma.

"Oh," Bitterroot said, "I don't count that Cree squaw I had. Don't count that concubine I had in Bannack City, either. Her name was Karen. Green eyes. Full of soul. She was a full woman, all woman, kind of woman. . . . Well, you're too young to know of such things. I had her, though. Married her. And let some tinhorn from Saint Paul steal her from me."

The horses snorted. I could see their breath. No sound for the next mile except the wind.

"Yes, you're damned right," Bitterroot said when we neared the line shack. "Major MacDunn's got mighty good reasons for fighting to keep what's rightfully his."

Nothing left for us to do but ride back to the ranch, tell Major MacDunn what had happened. Gene Hardee had gathered up his bunch of wire stringers, and we all returned to the Bar DD, leaving behind a few worthless miles of wire fence.

'Course, me being so young, I wasn't privy

to the conversation between Gene Hardee, Major MacDunn, and Bitterroot Abbott. Didn't really want to hear what was being said. Didn't really want to have to talk to Lainie, but she cornered me in the barn.

"Tommy quit." That was the first thing she said to me. "He just rode off in the middle of the night."

I put my saddle on the peg, turned, saw she'd been crying. Probably crying since Tommy up and lit a shuck.

"Have you seen him?" she asked me.

"He write any letters?" Dumb thing to ask, and you wouldn't have heard any sympathy in my voice, but I had to know for sure.

"What?"

"Before he left. He write any letters? Other than the one I wrote for him."

She blinked. "Mother said he gave one to Frank Raleigh when Father sent him to Helena."

Frank Raleigh was a quiet cowhand for the Bar DD. First fellow I ever saw wearing woolly chaps.

"Why?" she said. "Why did you ask that?"

"No reason," I lied. That settled things for me, though, truthfully. I already knew Tommy had told the railroad officials what the hackers were doing on the sly.

"Did you see him? Where would he have gone?"

I let out a deep breath, trying to think how to answer.

"He thinks he's a monster!" She started crying again.

"Tommy just. . . ." The words came hard for me. "He just needs . . . to . . . sort things out. For himself."

She shut off those tears, looked up at me. "I guess I do, too," she said.

I had things to sort out myself.

Weather turned colder, wind blew harder, skies turned grayer. Gene Hardee sent us out to cowboy, but he kept a lot of folks at the ranch headquarters. Bunkhouse filled up with all sorts of cowboys. Frank Raleigh. A man of color named Greene. Frenchy Hurault, the Métis. Busted-Tooth Melvin and Paul Scott. And a lot of guys whose names I can't remember. And me, of course, and Walter Butler, Ish Fishtorn, and Camdan Gow.

Bitterroot Abbott wasn't there, though. The major had sent him down to Helena the day after we rode back. It wasn't till later that I learned why he had gone.

It was just a bad time. Gloomy. I got to punch some cattle, check on water holes, work on the back of a horse — things I was good at, even gentle a few rangy bronc's. Only my heart wasn't in it. I felt sad, and lonely.

Seemed that everybody in the Bar DD bunkhouse felt the same way.

Waiting for a war.

Ish would clean that big Centennial rifle just about every night, and other hired men did the same, oiling their pistols — if they owned a revolver — or rifles, filling the empty loops in their shell belts.

Waiting for the war.

I felt bad for Camdan Gow.

He was still on the Bar DD, doing chores. Nobody talked to him. It ain't that they treated him like a prisoner, but more like they just pretended he wasn't around. Except for Mrs. MacDunn. She was always protecting him, keeping him safe, making sure he didn't hear what was being said about his daddy.

But Camdan wasn't deaf, wasn't stupid. He knew. He was just a good boy, didn't cotton to violence. Just like his old man.

The wind blew cold.

The morning they came, a couple of days after we turned the bulls loose, I was in the corral, working hard with a currycomb on

Crabtown. His coat was a mess, just thick, unruly, like he was some rangy mustang running wild in the mountains.

"Major MacDunn!" Busted-Tooth Melvin called out, and I heard the pounding of hoofs. Well, I dropped that currycomb, scrambled up the corral, and just froze there, perched on the top rail, when Mr. Gow rode up with a half dozen men. They reined up near the main house, Tommy and John Henry closest to me.

Ish Fishtorn and a couple of boys walked from the bunkhouse, Ish holding that big rifle at the ready. Other men stayed by the bunkhouse, where they could fine shelter. Me? I had no place to hide. If folks started shooting, I figured I was dead.

Seemed like a month passed before Major MacDunn walked outside, a double-action revolver in his right hand, cocked, but the barrel hanging alongside his leg.

Camdan Gow ran from the bunkhouse, and nobody tried to stop him. He pulled up right beside his daddy, who looked as if he had aged ten years since last I saw him.

Mrs. MacDunn stepped through the doorway.

"Get inside, Blaire!" the major barked.

Mrs. MacDunn stepped out, away from

her husband, defying him, and the major's ears started turning redder than mine ever did.

Then Lainie ran out of the house, stopping beside her mother. Even from where I was, I could tell they'd both been crying.

Time passed. We waited for the war to commence.

As the wind blew cold.

CHAPTER NINETEEN

Mr. Gow made the first move, reaching inside the coat of his Mackinaw, stopping for a moment when Major MacDunn started to raise his pistol barrel. John Henry put his hand on the butt of his revolver. So did a couple other of Gow's men, and Ish eared back the hammer of his Winchester.

I tried to swallow, but didn't have nothing in my throat but a dry, cold dread.

Mr. Gow's and the major's eyes locked, and slowly Gow withdrew a fringed elk-hide pouch, which he tossed at the major's boots. I heard the jingle of coin when the pouch landed in the dirt.

"I owe you, William, for damages to your fence. I trust you will find that sufficient."

Looking a bit surprised, Major MacDunn lowered the revolver, but kept it cocked, kept his finger in the trigger guard.

"I had nothing to do with that wanton destruction, William. These two. . . ." He shot a quick glance in Tommy and John Henry's directions. "Well, they took matters into their own hands. For their own reasons."

Mr. Gow wet his lips. John Henry and Tommy just stared ahead, not blinking, barely breathing.

"I pray we may discuss matters in private, William. As civilized men."

"Get off my land." I could barely hear the major. His fingers tightened against the revolver's butt.

Mrs. MacDunn gasped, and the major glared at his wife, then looked back at Mr. Gow with cruel eyes.

"Your land?" Mr. Gow let out a hollow laugh. "This so-called MacDunn Empire is open range. You're nothing more than a general manager, serving at the pleasure of the board of directors, and the shareholders, of the Dee and Don Rivers Land and Cattle Company. I have written a formal complaint to Sir Alistair Shaw in Aberdeen. You might not have a job by spring."

"My land." The major lifted the revolver again, ignoring his wife's plea. "I said get off."

"We have always had an understanding, William. This is open range."

"Which I control."

"I do not detest barbed wire, William. You have every right to fence off some pasture. I understand that Granville Stuart has done the same in the Judith Basin. Barbed wire fences are no longer only for farmers. Many Texas ranchers are protecting their water holes, some pasture."

"Get out of my sight!"

"For God's sake, William. I pray for peace. After the fire, after . . . well . . . I sent Camdan back here, after arduous discussion with my wife, hoping his presence would alleviate any tension. . . ." He took a deep breath, and slowly exhaled. "William, we were friends in Scotland."

"This is not Aberdeen!"

"The range you chose to fence is range that we agreed the Bar DD and the Seven-Three Connected would share. I needed that land after the fire. You knew that. You could have. . . ."

"This is not about land, you fool!"

Mr. Gow gripped his saddle horn, his face masked by bewilderment. His horse pranced nervously. Another one of his riders — the colored man who had driven Mrs. Gow to the Bar DD to get help during the fire — let his hand drop near the rifle in his scabbard.

Mr. Gow's Adam's apple bobbed.

"Please, William. Allow us to talk privately." He glanced at Camdan, then at Lainie. He made himself look away from Mrs. MacDunn.

I guess the major realized Mr. Gow wasn't a fighting man. Suddenly he laughed, lowering the hammer on his Bulldog revolver, shoving it inside his waistband.

"Tristram, I don't blame you at all. Your own wife's turned crazy as a loon."

Now, Mr. Gow's face flushed.

"It's lonely country," the major said, grinning without humor. "It is not like Scotland."

Suddenly Tommy shot me a hard look.

The crooked smile vanished from the major's face. "But you come here fancying my wife!"

Groaning, Mrs. MacDunn took a step toward the major, but Lainie saw that look in her father's eyes, a look that scared her, and she grabbed her mother's arm, pulled her back.

"William," Mr. Gow pleaded.

"Don't call me William. I should kill you right now."

He sounded sadder, older, worn out, Mr. Gow did, when he spoke again. "I am sorry if I have led you to believe. . . . I . . . it is not fair to Blaire to. . . ."

"Missus MacDunn, Gow. She's Missus MacDunn to you!"

Another eternity passed.

"Mister Gow?" the black rider asked. He was ready and willing to pull his rifle, and draw blood.

Mr. Gow's head shook tiredly. "I have never desired anything from your wife except her friendship," he said, and this time he turned to look at Mrs. MacDunn. "I am sorry if I led you to believe otherwise. She is a friend. A dear friend. As you once were, William." He looked back at the major. "But I love my wife. I love my family. And I love what I have tried to carve in this wilderness for them."

He looked down at his son. "Catch up your horse, Camdan. It is time we go home. Quickly, Son."

"I have seen enough bloodshed on this frontier," Mr. Gow said when Camdan had disappeared inside the barn. "I had prayed you would have, too, after those lynchings a few years back. I detest violence. You know that. There will be no war on the Sun and Teton Rivers, Major MacDunn. At least, I shall not start it. I will find winter grass elsewhere. In Canada. If it's not too late."

He shot his arm out toward Tommy and John Henry.

"These men admitted to me their handi-work in the ruination of your fence. I have fired Kenton, have banished them from my range. Yet I trust you will show mercy, will not press charges. There is enough money in that pouch to replace your precious wire. The boy, I believe, has been hurt enough."

Camdan rode out of the barn, and Mr. Gow tipped his hat at Mrs. MacDunn. Her lips mouthed the words — "I am sorry." — and the 7-3 Connected riders loped away, disappearing over the hills, leaving behind John Henry and Tommy, whose horses took a few nervous steps, wanting to run after the other riders, wanting to get away from the Bar DD.

I felt the same way.

What happened? Nothing. Not really. Well, maybe everything.

My heart pounded against my ribs, but I could breathe again. We watched the dust fade, then John Henry, his hand still on the butt of his revolver, turned toward Major MacDunn.

"Well?" His words were icy. "What's your play?"

The major stared at him, started to look at either his wife or daughter — I'm not sure which — but stopped.

"Get out of my sight," the major said. "If I ever find you on MacDunn range, I will hang you both. Jim Hawkins!"

I like to have toppled off the rail.

"Yes, sir?" Surprised I could even talk.

"If you want to ride off with your friends, get your war bag and saddle, and be gone."

Which was all I needed to hear. I jumped down, started for the bunkhouse to get my possibles, get out of Montana, make things right between John Henry and Tommy and me. Too stupid, too green to know any better.

"No!"

John Henry's voice stopped me. Turning around, I looked up at my two pards.

"You ain't fit to ride with John Henry Kenton," John Henry said, leaning forward in his saddle. "I ride with pards I can trust, not some back-stabbing son-of-a-bitch who'd steal my pard's girl."

"John Henry," I pleaded, and felt tears welling in my eyes. "Tommy, I ain't. . . ."

"We left Texas, boy," John Henry said, "to get away from the wire. You forgot that. You put a pick in your hands like some miserable sodbuster, nailed the devil's rope to fence posts. And look what you did to Tommy. Your friend! I hold you responsible."

My head fell to my chest. The tears dried up, but I knew John Henry was right. Right about most things — about me forgetting, about me being responsible for Tommy's injuries. But he was dead wrong about me ever trying to steal Lainie from him. I liked her a lot, but I'd never do a pard like that. Never do anyone that way.

"Get off my land," Major MacDunn said with a quiet authority. "Both of you. And remember my warning."

I heard John Henry's words. "Oh, I'll remember them, MacDunn, but you remember this. You look long and hard at what you did to Tommy. You study his face. Because the ball has just started."

Hoofs sounded. Footsteps walked away. I stood there several minutes, not knowing what to do, felt a presence before me, and knew it was Lainie. I looked up into her tear-filled eyes.

"I'm sorry, Jim," she said.

"Ain't your fault," I told her.

Beyond her, I saw that elk-skin pouch, still in the dirt, where the major had left it.

Oh, I reckon the major later got that money. Don't think he left it for Busted-Tooth Melvin to steal. Don't know for sure, though, because snow covered the ground by evening.

Ain't what you figured, is it, boy? Certainly, it ain't the way they'd make it happen in one of those moving-picture deals they show down in Helena. No big shoot-out. Hardly a gun even cocked. No cowboys lying dead in the dust.

No heroes, either.

There was no range war, not between the MacDunns and the Gows. We went back to cowboying, not preparing to kill people.

I think about that. Have thought about it often. How things changed. I think about how blind we were. All of us. We didn't notice, didn't pay attention to all the signs, didn't think about what was happening all around us. We was all too concerned about barbed wire, and a dead bull, and winter grass, and Mrs. MacDunn. And Lainie. We kept considering what we'd wind up doing, or how we'd act, who'd live and who'd die, when that first trigger got pulled.

Nobody, not me, not John Henry, not Major MacDunn or Mr. Gow or Gene Hardee or Bitterroot Abbott saw what was happening. Not a one of us thought about why a grizzly would come out of its range hunting horses to eat, or why its coat growed so thick. Or why Angus bulls started sporting hair like you'd find on a buffalo. Or why those black bulls started acting so unpredictable, certainly not the calm beasts they was supposed to be. Or why geese flew south long before normal. Why the other birds vanished. Or why a cottonwood tree's bark got so thick. Why the wind blew so cold. Why our horses also grew winter coats so early.

Why beavers worked harder than even beavers was supposed to work. Or why muskrats took to making their homes on the creeks twice as big as they usually did.

Oh, there was a war coming, sure enough. Only it come from another direction. And it would have every last one of us, from the Bar DD to the 7-3 Connected, from the Judith Basin to Miles City, across all of Montana and the Dakotas and Wyoming and beyond. . . .

Have every one of us fighting to hold on.

Fighting to stay alive.

CHAPTER TWENTY

In the early dusk, they cross the shallow waters at a bend in the Sun River, letting their horses pick their paths over smooth, slippery stones, then push through the brush toward the cañon's high wall. It's here that Jim Hawkins and his grandson make camp, using driftwood on the river's edge to build a fire, warming themselves against spring's chill.

"It's near abouts," Henry Lancaster hears his grandfather say. "It's got to be around here. If I can find the place. . . ."

Without another word, Jim Hawkins pulls a lengthy piece of twisted wood from the fire and, using it as a torch, makes his way through the brush, holding the blaze close to the cañon's limestone walls. Quietly Henry follows.

His grandfather looks intently at the wall, bringing the torch closer, then moving along, finally reaching an overhang, and ducking inside the natural shelter. His boots brush back weeds and stones, revealing nothing, and, sighing, he lifts the torch toward the ceiling.

"See those?" Jim Hawkins asks Henry.

"Yes, sir."

Small hand prints dot the limestone wall, like wallpaper patterns, the color of dried blood. Some are smeared, others so clear, Henry can picture someone pressing his hand against the stone.

"Who made them?" the boy asks, then chances a guess. "You?"

"No," Jim Hawkins answers. "Some Indians. Don't know how long ago. Before I got to Montana. Before I was even born. Maybe even before my pa was born. Who knows?"

Henry thinks he sees other drawings on the wall, figures of some kind, perhaps drawings of Indians holding shields, maybe a spear. It's hard to tell in the fading light. He wonders what they mean.

For a few minutes, Jim Hawkins kicks around in the natural shelter, lowering the flame, searching the rubble, finding nothing.

"Ain't nothing here," he says. "Hell, there was nothing here then, neither." He looks back at the hand prints. "Except those."

"When?" the boy asks. "When?"

Jim Hawkins doesn't answer. He steps out, begins moving back to camp. The flame on *the torch is dying.*

Again his grandson follows.

When they reach camp, Hawkins tosses the stick in the center of the pit, squats by the fire, holds his gloved hands out to warm them. A coffee pot rests on a flat stone, the smell of the strong brew reminding Henry of how long it has been since he has eaten. The horses snort. The river ripples. An owl hoots. Henry Lancaster kneels beside his grandfather.

"I guess I owe you the rest of the story," Jim Hawkins says. "Ain't given you much lately, just some bits and pieces, way things I remember them. But you deserve an ending. And all of it. Lainie knows most of it, but not everything."

The flames illuminate Jim Hawkins's weathered face. His eyes don't seem to blink. He wets his lips, lowers his hands, finally sits back.

Henry watches, waiting, unsure.

"Kissin-ey-oo-way'-o," his grandfather begins in a whisper. "The wind blows cold."

Winter, 1886–87

Winter in Montana seldom begins before the First of January, and extreme cold scarcely ever lasts more than two or three days at a time. . . . Still, for Montana's flocks and herds, much depends on the coming winter.

— *Great Falls Tribune,*
December 18, 1886

CHAPTER
TWENTY-ONE

I awoke in the bunkhouse, shivering underneath my blankets. Just the sound of the wind turned my blood cold. The bunkhouse seemed to be creaking, moaning. Felt like another gust would send the entire log building sailing all the way to eternity.

November 16, 1886.

First thing I saw was Old Man Woodruff x-ing off the date on the calendar tacked up next to a tintype of some girl — nobody remembered who she was or who stuck the picture on the wall — near the stove.

The door swung open, and the wind blasted us, as Old Man Woodruff directed some prime cuss words toward Ish Fishtorn. How hard was the wind whipping? Well, it took both Ish and Frank Raleigh to get that door shut.

"Is it snowing?" I asked sleepily.

"Too cold to snow," Ish answered.

That brutal wind would cut you deep,

freeze the marrow in your bones. Felt that way, anyhow. The temperature dropped to two degrees below zero, and gray clouds blocked out the sun. Most times, it might get cold in Montana, but if the sky remains clear, the sun feels warm. Twenty degrees didn't always feel so miserable when the sun showed itself. But two below zero, with the wind tearing across the hills at better than fifty miles an hour, well, there was no sun, no heat, just relentless cold.

Too cold to snow?

Not hardly.

The blizzard struck the next morning. November 17th. Made me almost forget about the killing storm that struck Texas some ten months earlier.

Reluctantly I dragged myself from beneath the covers again to the smell of coffee and bacon, and the roaring, unrelenting wind. Once I found my boots, I realized it had to be well past dawn. Wasn't nobody in the bunkhouse except Busted-Tooth Melvin, a still-snoring Walter Butler, me, and an ice-covered cowhand who stood by the stove stamping snow off his boots. They'd let me and Walter sleep in, seemed like, and that riled me. I expected to do a day's work for a day's pay, like everybody else, had been doing that since I came to this country, and

I didn't like being treated like some green pea. Oh, them boys meant well, still thinking of me and Walter as kids, but I'd show them. So would Walter. I hollered at him to get up, that daylight was fading.

Fading? It felt like the sun kept moving farther and farther away. Looked like early dawn or dusk, even at high noon, the next two days.

As I went to pour my first cup of coffee, I eyed the man who'd just come in from the storm. Slowly he revealed himself to me as he unwrapped a long woolen scarf that he had looped over his hat, pulling the brim down over his ears. His beard was crusted white, his nose red. Gene Hardee swore again while shedding his coat.

"Hope you got a gallon of coffee, Woody," Hardee said. " 'Cause I aim to drink it all. It ain't frozen, is it, Jim?"

I filled his cup.

"How long has it been snowing?" I asked.

"Since September, feels like. Ain't like those dustings we've had. Ain't like anything you've ever seen."

"You wasn't in Texas in January," I told him.

He grunted. Didn't believe me. Didn't believe it ever got cold in Texas. I let him remain ignorant.

Fortified with some stout Folgers, I headed back to my bunk, fetched my shirt, pulled my shirt over my head, and grabbed my hat.

"Where is everybody?" Walter asked with a big yawn.

"Working." Hardee rubbed some feeling back into his nose. "Stupid cattle. A horse is fair smart. Smart enough to forage for food. A horse'll eat snow when it can't find any water, but a cow'll just founder and die in belly-deep snow."

"We best get after them," I told Walter Butler, grabbing my heavy coat, and headed for the door. Good, loyal Walter followed me.

"Where you two goin'?" Busted-Tooth Melvin said.

"I earn my keep," I told him.

Walter said: "I got to visit the privy."

Gene Hardee piped in, "Not like that, kiddoes."

I didn't like that word. Kiddoes. It was what John Henry always called me and Tommy. I kept right for the door.

Gene Hardee cut me off. Shaking his head, he opened the door, let me see just what that storm was doing. Just briefly, mind you, but long enough to get another scolding from Melvin. I saw nothing but white. Then Hardee pressed himself against the door, got it closed, and sent me and Walter back to our bunks.

"You break a leg," Hardee said, "you don't want to freeze to death lying on the ground. Got to dress you proper."

Well, Hardee and Melvin rigged me up so that I could hardly move, and done the same for Walter. Four pairs of socks, two of them thick woolies, and one of them stretching all the way over my knees — Dutch socks, Hardee called them — flannel underwear pulled up over my summer muslins, and an itchy undershirt, too, my duck trousers, and a heavy wool bib-front shirt. And my boots, of course. That wasn't all, neither. Though I already felt like I'd put on more clothes than I'd ever owned in all my years, Gene Hardee sat at the table, nursing coffee while using a pair of scissors on . . . well . . . it still kind of embarrasses me, all these years later. . . .

Ladies undergarments. Black, thin, real fancy. And soft.

"What are those?" Walter Butler said.

"Cashmere hose," Hardee said, handing me my pair and going to work on another pair for Walter.

"Hose?" Walter wailed, and I looked at the unmentionables in my hands. "You mean for a woman's . . . limbs?"

Busted-Tooth Melvin snorted so hard, he sent a bunch of spit flying between his missing front teeth, causing the stove to sizzle.

"Put them on your arms." Hardee said and tossed Walter his pair. "Use them as extra sleeves."

"Uhn-uh!" Walter dropped those black hose like they were rattlesnakes. "I'm not putting a woman's underwear on my arms!"

I just stared at mine. Hardee had cut out the feet.

"You'll do like a say, Walter. It's not going to get any warmer for quite a while, and, if you lose your arms up to your elbows because of frostbite, Missus MacDunn'll never let me hear the end of it."

I started to pull one of the things over my right arm, while Walter reluctantly picked up his pair.

"Where'd you get a pair of cashmere hose?" I asked.

"Two pairs," Busted-Tooth Melvin corrected, spitting on the stove again.

Gene Hardee grinned. "Utica," he finally answered. "Stole them from a couple of. . . ."

"Poor, distressed ladies," Melvin chimed in.

Hardee finished his coffee. "Wouldn't call

them ladies."

"Nuns," Melvin said. "Nuns from Saint Peter's Mission."

Walter dropped the hose on the floor again, and I thought both Hardee and Melvin would die.

"Nuns don't wear cashmere hose," I told those men. I knew they were funning us.

I also knew what kind of women Hardee had been visiting in Utica.

Wasn't finished dressing, yet. Put on overalls — looked like I was nothing but a poor granger — and chaps, my gloves, and a mask Melvin had made for me by cutting out the inside lining of an old coat. You wouldn't recognize me. Felt like I was a bandit about to rob a bank. Wrapped my bandanna over my head the way Gene Hardee had done, pulling the brim of my hat down over my ears. Walter was luckier. He had a cap made of sealskin to keep his ears warm. He also had a pair of big over-shoes instead of stovepipe leather boots.

Thus fortified, we stepped outside.

And like to have froze to death.

This was like no wind that ever blew, the most vicious gale, carrying with it the screams of thousands and thousands and thousands of men and women and animals and monsters. Like it came from the depths of hell, only with a numbing cold instead of the worst heat, filling the air with snow that stabbed like rock salt fired from a shotgun.

It slashed. It cut. It tore. It wailed.

No matter how many layers of clothing Gene Hardee and Busted-Tooth Melvin put on me, it wasn't enough. Nothing could protect you from that icy fury.

When I think about it, the snow didn't really amount to much. Not then. The big storms came later. That November day, I'd guess we got six inches, maybe seven, but the wind kept whipping it around. It felt more like riding through a West Texas sandstorm than a snowstorm. Those Aberdeen Angus cattle, black as midnight, were easy to spot in the wailing, gray-tinted whiteness. That was our one bit of good fortune, but the cattle hadn't gotten used to this range, and they'd drift, and bawl, and drift, and moan, and drift, and drift, and drift. Snow drifted, too, piling high against the walls of the ranch buildings, producing mounds scattered on the wind-swept, snow-covered hills that surrounded the Bar DD headquarters.

Heads bent low, hands stuck deep in our coat pockets, reins hanging around saddle horns, me and Walter, Gene Hardee, and Busted-Tooth Melvin pushed some Angus and longhorn toward something that might resemble a shelter. Finding a windbreak in Montana proved mighty hard.

I didn't see the accident. Didn't even hear it. If Busted-Tooth Melvin hadn't been paying attention, we might would have left our boss lying in the snow to die, but Melvin kept yelling, and finally the wind blew his shouts in my direction. I pulled my hands out of the pockets, took the reins, stopped Crabtown, and shouted hard at Walter Butler. Walter was riding right beside me, but the wind cried so loud, blew so hard, it took me four or five good whoops before he heard me, and reined up. I pointed, and we turned our mounts, rode into that brutal wind, and saw what had happened.

Gene was standing, hopping, favoring his left leg, trying to catch the reins of the buckskin, which was lying on the snow. He yelled something. Couldn't hear it. Couldn't hear anything. Saw Busted-Tooth Melvin's head shake.

"Get down!" Busted-Tooth Melvin made a motion with his hands, and me and Walter swung from our mounts, watching Melvin pull a Marlin repeater from the scabbard.

Next he handed me the reins to his clay-bank.

"For God's sake, boy," he said, and I could just barely hear him, "don't drop these reins! Keep between the horses. That'll protect you from the wind. And hold 'em reins tight. Tight! You hear me?"

I wasn't green. Knew if I let any horse wander off, we'd be in a bad fix. My head bobbed, and I started to pull off one of my gloves, so I could get a better hold on the stiff, cold leather, but Melvin stopped me *pronto*.

"You want to lose 'em fingers?" he barked. "Keep that glove on!"

Gene Hardee hopped over to us, while Melvin slowly worked the lever of his rifle.

"You all right?" Melvin asked.

Had to yell it again before Gene Hardee could hear.

"Twisted my ankle!" He hooked a heavy mitten thumb toward the horse, still writhing in the snowbank. "Sprained it. Or something. Horse stumbled in the bank!"

"I'll see to it!" Melvin stepped toward the downed animal.

I saw, too. Saw the blood pouring from the buckskin's two front legs, the wind blowing what looked like small cherries. That's how fast the blood froze. A crimson lake of ice already stained the snowdrift while the horse screamed and tried to stand, but couldn't.

Cold and the wind had turned snowdrifts into ragged knives of ice, and, when Gene Hardee's horse stumbled, the drift tore away the flesh, carved rugged slices all the way to the cannon bones. The left leg had snapped, terribly, pushing a ragged edge of bone through the battered, bloody skin.

Suddenly the buckskin's head slammed into the snowbank, shuddering, gave one last violent kick, then lay still, quiet, its big eye glazing over. I didn't even hear the report of Melvin's rifle, didn't see smoke from the barrel. The horses just stood calmly, too cold, too scared, too miserable to catch the scent of blood. Like the rest of us, they heard just the howling wind.

Melvin returned the rifle to the scabbard. "Jim!" he said. "Get Gene back to the bunkhouse! Don't tarry! Don't look directly at the snow! But watch where you're goin'!"

He waited to make sure I understood, then told Hardee what he was doing, that he and Walter Butler would take care of the cattle. We helped our boss into the saddle, and before Melvin mounted his horse, he grabbed my wrist again, looking up from the ground, his eyebrows caked with frosted icy. "Stay clear of the snowdrifts! Let your horse pick its path! Likely he knows the way back to the ranch better than you! Can you do this, Jim?"

I nodded.

"Good boy! I'll see you back at the ranch!"

We waited till Melvin mounted, watched him and a trembling Walter Butler ride into the big emptiness, then I made for the Bar DD. Last thing I remember seeing was Gene Hardee's buckskin, already covered with snow.

CHAPTER
TWENTY-TWO

Crabtown got us back to the Bar DD, but, when Mrs. MacDunn seen us, she give Hardee both barrels of her Scottish tongue while helping me help him into the bunkhouse.

"A boy Jim's age shouldn't be risking his life for foolish men like you and my hardheaded husband. Jim Hawkins and Walter Butler should be in school!" she said.

"They're in school, ma'am," Gene told her. "My school."

Mrs. MacDunn muttered something I couldn't catch, and we eased Gene Hardee onto his bunk. "What happened?" she demanded.

"Oh, twisted my ankle is all. Sprained it. Lost my horse." He didn't go into details as to what exactly had happened to his horse.

"You should put some ice on it," she said. "Keep the swelling down."

"Good thing there's plenty of ice handy,"

Gene said.

Not appreciating his humor, she gave him a stare colder than it was outside before sending me out to fetch some ice.

Turned out, though, that Gene Hardee hadn't twisted or sprained his ankle. He had busted the bone pretty good. Had to use a butcher knife to cut off his boot, and I think that irritated him as much as being an invalid. Those boots had cost him $15 in Helena, and he was none to happy to ruin one of them. 'Course, we didn't have no hard plaster to fix up a cast, but Mrs. Mac-Dunn and me got the bone set, braced with some slats from Camdan Gow's old bunk, and she fixed him some willow bark tea to help ease the pain.

Gene Hardee was the first casualty that winter.

Next morning, I dabbed charcoal underneath my eyes to cut down on the glare from the snow, and went outside, still bundled up against the biting cold. Forked hay to the animals in the corral and barn, and met Lainie at the woodpile, me fetching a load for the bunkhouse, and her getting some for her home. Hadn't seen her much of late, and couldn't hardly recognize her wearing her pa's overcoat and overshoes. I told her

I'd carry the wood for her, but she just stared past me. Not sure she even heard my offer, or even recognized me.

Then she asked: "Jim, what kind of bird is that?"

I turned, following where she was pointing. It was hard to spot in that snow, but I found it at last atop the barn.

Big bird, I mean to tell you, maybe two feet long. The color of snow, but with a fair amount of black, and feathers all the way down to the feet. The face was pure white, except for its big black beak, but what really struck me were those eyes, a cold, penetrating yellow. It took off just a few seconds later, and I'd never seen a wing span like that on no owl, which is what I had taken it for. Some kind of owl, a white owl, a big owl.

Later, I'd see two more of them birds — one with no dark splotches, at all, I mean completely white — except for that black beak and jaundice eyes — with heavy feathers. Nobody had ever seen those owls, except Frenchy Hurault, and that old Métis shook his head sadly when he saw another big owl that evening.

"Mon Dieu," he whispered, talking to the big bird. "You are far from home."

A bird from the Arctic, a snowy owl. Flying south.

"A bad omen," Frenchy said.

All night, we heard that owl's haunting call.

Pyee! Pyee! Pyee!
Prek! Prek! Prek!
Pyee!

Until the wind started howling again.

Within a few days, however, the temperatures warmed, and the drifts of snow grew smaller, yet the hills surrounding the Bar DD remained a barren expanse of white, of crusted snow. Dark clouds became a fixture over the Rocky Mountains.

"What we need," Ish Fishtorn said, "is The Black Wind to take care. . . ."

"You will have a long wait before you see your first Chinook," Old Man Woodruff said, rubbing his left knee. "That's what these joints of mine tell me." He sighed. "I never should have left Florida."

Walter Butler came down with snow blindness, hurting something terrible. We put him to bed, and Old Man Woodruff laid salt poultices over his eyes, but Walter acted like a wild man, throwing those off, begging for us to kill him. Had to tie his arms and legs to the cot. You wouldn't think snow blindness would do that to a fellow. We kept those salt poultices on him for three, four days, but Walter could hardly eat or drink, he was hurting so bad.

Finally Mrs. MacDunn brought over a small bottle of Perry Davis Pain Killer, but she sounded skeptical.

"I've heard this works," she said. "But I am not sure."

Well, we removed the poultices, and got ready. Ish Fishtorn pulled back one of Walter's eyelids, and Mrs. MacDunn let a few drops fall into his left eye. Most of the liquid dribbled down Walter's face, but a couple of drops must have hit the mark, because that boy started screaming, pulling at his sheets we'd used to tie him to his bed, cussing up a storm. Walter Butler wasn't known for having such a foul mouth, and I felt glad that Major MacDunn wasn't around to hear what that boy was calling Mrs. MacDunn. Felt gladder, I'll admit, that Walter had the snowblindness, and not me.

Proved even harder to get those last drops into Walter's other eye, but we done it, and Walter's shrieks like to have blowed down the bunkhouse walls.

Cured him, though. Don't know if it was the painkiller or the salt poultices, but Walter's eyes got better, though they were redder than my ears got for a few days. Too bad Mrs. MacDunn didn't have anything to cure Frank Raleigh's frostbite.

He come down with that riding over toward Castle Reef to check on things. Come back complaining that he couldn't feel anything with his fingertips on his left hand. Come back with some news, too. More fence — the section on the northern side of Castle Reef — had been torn down. John Henry and Tommy's work, we knew, but nobody said anything about it. Nobody said anything to Major MacDunn about the dead Angus bull that Frank Raleigh had found tangled in the coils of barbed wire by the destroyed fence.

"Wolves had already gotten to him by the time I come upon him," Frank Raleigh said, rubbing his fingers. "Might have been dead before the wolves got him. Or the wolves might have drove him into the wire. No way to know. You plan on telling the major?"

Sitting on his bunk, broken ankle propped up with a pillow, Gene Hardee shook his head. "He'll learn about it come spring. No point in starting another war. Suspect we'll lose a few more head before the Chinooks come."

"Reckon so," Raleigh said.

"An eye for an eye," Hardee whispered,

not meaning for anybody to hear him, but Frank Raleigh was right there.

"And a bull for a bull?" he asked.

Gene Hardee didn't answer, and Raleigh went to his bunk, massaging his purple fingers.

Old Man Woodruff had him stop rubbing those fingers, told him to soak them in a bowl of hot water, and Frank did that, but it was too late, although he told us his fingers didn't hurt any more. Wasn't long after that, though, that the tips of three fingers on his left hand, just above the first joints, started looking like wood twigs, and the purple started turning black.

That's when Frank Raleigh got good and drunk from a bottle Paul Scott gave him, and, as Busted-Tooth Melvin held his hand down on the table, Old Man Woodruff cut off the frostbit fingers with a knife, and cauterized the ends.

Thanksgiving came and went without notice.

I wasn't particularly hungry anyhow.

CHAPTER
TWENTY-THREE

The weather seemed to break for us. Oh, those clouds to the west still threatened something awful, and icy snow refused to melt, but the storms had passed, even the wind died down to something tolerable. Besides, thirty degrees don't feel so bad after days in single digits, and nights even colder.

With his hand mangled, Frank Raleigh said he planned on wintering with his sister down in Laramie. Hoped it would be warmer in Wyoming, he said, and give him time to get used to not having all of his fingers. It might have been pride, though, him being shamed with his bad hand, or it might have been the fact that, as Ish Fishtorn later suggested, there were a whole lot more saloons in Laramie than on the Sun River.

Like I said, we didn't celebrate Thanksgiving. Not like anyone could find a turkey to shoot, but I never felt so thankful as that December afternoon when Tommy O'Hallahan rode back to the Bar DD.

He was sprouting whiskers, just saplings, mind you, but I hadn't noticed them before. Couldn't help but notice when he rode up, though, what with the fuzz on his face caked with ice. Must have been riding quite a while, and he looked more like a cadaver than a cowboy.

I'd just come out of the barn, walking through the path we'd made in the snow to the bunkhouse. Major MacDunn stood on the bunkhouse porch with Gene Hardee, our foreman on his crutches, the major smoking a pipe. The major set the pipe aside, and stood straighter when he recognized the rider. I hadn't even noticed, but turned around when I heard the horse snort. My jaw opened, my breath an icy mist.

I stopped.

He rode Midnight Beauty, a woolen scarf wrapped around his hat and chin, warming his good ear.

The major swore, and I looked back at the bunkhouse, my heart thudding against my ribs, as my boss brushed back his long black greatcoat, and put his gloved hand on a holstered revolver. Only before Major

MacDunn stepped down or pulled his pistol, Gene Hardee started talking.

"MacDunn," Hardee said, "you pull that pistol, you'll eat it."

No Major. No Mister. Just MacDunn. Tell you something, boy. I'd never been prouder of Gene Hardee than I was at that moment, standing up to his boss like that. Never been so surprised as when the major let Hardee's remarks pass, took his hand away from the Bulldog revolver, and tightened the coat around his waist again.

Gene Hardee hobbled on the crutches through the icy path, and stopped beside me. We waited for Tommy. A moment later, the major walked over, and stood behind us. I could hear his heavy breathing.

Tommy reined up, and looked down.

"You riding the grubline, son?" Hardee asked. "Or looking for a job?"

"I don't think many outfits are hiring this time of year," Tommy said.

"You might be in luck. One of my hands lost some fingers to frostbite. He'd been at the line camp at Sun River Cañon. He quit, so I need a good cowboy."

MacDunn grunted.

Tommy wet his frozen lips.

"Are you riding this country alone?" the major said. "Or do you have a partner?"

Tommy swallowed. "I'm alone."

"Certain of that?"

"Yes, sir."

After clearing his throat, Major MacDunn told Gene Hardee he'd leave the hiring up to him, then, head bent, he walked back to his house.

"You don't have to make your mind up about the job yet," Hardee said. "Nobody ever left the Bar DD hungry. Tend your horse, and come inside. I'll warm up stew. Jim, you help him. Expect y'all have some catching up to do."

At first, we worked in silence, removing the saddle and bridle, rubbing down the grulla roan. Finally Tommy muttered an oath, and faced me. "You might as well ask your questions. I can see curiosity is tearing apart your stomach."

I didn't let him buffalo me. "Where's John Henry?" I asked.

"I don't know."

"Did you help him tear down that stretch of fence that Gene Hardee helped put up?"

He rubbed the corner of his eye patch. At first I thought he was reminding me of what wire had done to him, but then I realized he was just hurting. He patted Midnight Beauty, and stepped away. I followed him.

"It's one thing to tear down fence. . . ." His words died, and he let out a heavy sigh. "He's changed, Jim."

Tommy squatted by the barn door. I knelt across from him. The wind started to pick up.

"Yeah, I was with him," he admitted.

"I don't blame you," I said, just to say something. Well, I didn't blame him. Had my face been slashed up by that wire, likely I'd've done the same thing.

"But after. . . ." His head shook. "He's talking crazy, Jim."

I didn't interrupt, just knelt there, waiting.

"After we pulled down some fence, we rode to the line camp. You know, the one across the Sun River by the cañon?" My head slightly bobbed. The same camp Frank Raleigh had been working. The same camp where we'd worked when Tommy's bad accident happened. "Spent the night there, just to get out of the cold. I figured we'd light out, but, come first light, John Henry said we needed to visit the hackers up at Tie Camp Creek. So, we rode up there. John Henry asked to see the ramrod."

I pictured that thieving, whiskey-swilling coward named Burke.

"He almost beat him to death. The man

came in, and John Henry slammed his revolver barrel against his head. Just beat him, the poor man screaming till he was unconscious. Then the other workers came, and John Henry whirled. He didn't shoot anybody, though I suspect he would have if anyone had tried anything. Just threatened them, told them this was a personal matter, and we'd be gone. We mounted up, rode out at a high lope." Slowly Tommy stood. "I quit him."

I nodded.

"Quit him like a coward. He had a bottle of whiskey, which put him to sleep. We'd camped in some cave. Left him snoring. I just couldn't ride with him. You made the right choice, staying here."

Wasn't my choice. Yet I said: "Those hackers were cutting the fence posts for the Bar DD. John Henry just blamed them." I swallowed, staring at Tommy's eye patch. "For what happened to you. He was fighting for you. He was always fighting for us. Like that time at Doan's. Remember?"

Tommy shook his head. "It's more than that, Jim. He blames everybody, not just the hackers, not just MacDunn and you. Blames the railroad for freighting the wire to Montana. Blames the Stockgrowers Association for allowing it to happen. I quit him. Left him in the middle of the night like some sneak thief."

"You done what you needed to do. And John Henry'll come around." I quickly changed the subject. "You gonna take that job Gene Hardee told you about?"

He shrugged. "I guess so."

"Be lonely. Up there. All winter." I thought about Lainie.

"I could use some time to myself. Think about things." He started out, but stopped, turned back to me, and started: "I've been a handful. . . ."

"Forget it." I waved him off. "I've vexed you a time or thirty."

"More like three hundred." He forced a smile.

We walked to the bunkhouse together.

Two days later, he rode out to the Sun River Cañon line shack, leaving behind Midnight Beauty, who looked plumb tuckered out anyway. Tommy left riding a zebra dun, and pulling a pack mule and couple of mounts for his string. He never said anything to Lainie, and she never tried to talk to him. Ish Fishtorn told him to take care of himself, and Mrs. MacDunn made him promise that he would ride back down for Christmas. Said she planned on cooking a goose, and wouldn't hear of him spending the holiday up in that line shack alone.

He tipped his hat at her, give the silent Major MacDunn a quick nod, and rode out. Rode toward those mountains, and those black clouds.

CHAPTER
TWENTY-FOUR

I think it was the winter.

The wind, the cold and snow and darkness, the emptiness. Nothing feels as lonely as Montana in winter. Nothing looked as terrible as the winter of '86 and '87, like it would never end. All of that plays on your mind, and I think that's what affected John Henry. He had no love for barbed wire, and what happened to Tommy just pushed him farther, but, had it not been for that winter, I think John Henry would just have rode on. Like he did in Texas that spring. Rode off in search of something new, some new place, a new country to make him forget about what had happened, make him forget about how things in cattle country kept changing. Yeah, I think it was the winter.

After breakfast, we'd ride out from the Bar DD — all except Walter Butler, no longer blind from the snow, but still mending, still weak — and work the cattle, try to find spots where the snow wasn't too deep. Kept right on working.

Word come of a bad train wreck west of Helena, but nothing more about John Henry. Nothing about the Gows. Tell you the truth, I started to miss school. Oh, Mrs. MacDunn give me a *Reader,* told me I needed to keep up my education, and Lainie would still come over on Sunday evenings, and we'd practice some from *Treasure Island.* But I missed seeing all those other kids who had attended school. You grow a little restless, seeing nothing but a white horizon, seeing the same faces, hearing the same voices, the same jokes. December had just started, and winter stays a long time in this country.

When the next storm hit, we bundled ourselves up, and rode out, trying to keep the cows from drifting to the river. All those layers of clothes must have weighed a ton, but the wind still pierced our veins, and snow stung our eyes, about the only part of our bodies not covered with some kind of clothing. The temperature dropped to right at zero, and, after a few hours, you could hardly see anything but a wall of snow.

Ish Fishtorn rode up, yelled at me to turn back, that we needed to get back to the bunkhouse. That man wasn't about to get an argument from me, so we returned to the Bar DD, waiting for the blizzard to blow itself out.

It did, but not till two, three days had passed.

Another break came, and I got to suspicioning such turns in the weather. They'd get our hopes up, make us believe things would be all right, then winter would blast her chillsome fury again. Snow wasn't that deep, maybe five or seven inches, but it turned hard and icy, and drifts piled everywhere, and those drifts might reach four, maybe six feet high.

Well, one morning after I had coffee-ed up and went to fork hay into the corrals, I spied a rider. First visitor we'd had since Tommy rode up, and I watched him come, riding a black horse, all hunched over from the wind and bitter cold. Tommy had come up when it was thirty degrees, but on that morning it was right at seven, and the wind just tore through you. Didn't think anybody would be riding to the Bar DD for no social visit.

The man reined up in front of me, wearing green eyeglasses to protect him from snowblindness, covered in an ice-crusted buffalo robe, and a coyote-fur cap. I didn't recognize him until he spoke my name, said

I was just the fellow he had come to see.

"What you want with me?" I asked Bitter-root Abbott.

"I ain't talking to you out here, boy!" he snapped. "I got caught in this storm a day out of Helena, and, if I don't get some coffee and a hot stove, I'm apt to start shooting."

Pitchfork in hand, I led his horse into the barn, directed Bitterroot to the bunkhouse, said I'd be in directly after I saw to his horse. He studied me a moment. I couldn't see his eyes through them funny-looking glasses, but I could tell he wondered if I'd run off from him. Crazy notion. Like I'd go anywhere in this weather. Reckon he come to the same conclusion, because he left me with his dun horse, and I put the gaunt animal in a stall with some grain and water. Had to bust ice in the bucket so the poor animal could drink. Threw his saddle and traps on a peg, and walked to the bunkhouse to see what a gunman like Bitterroot Abbott wanted with a cowboy like me.

When I walked into the bunkhouse, Bitterroot had shed his big buffalo coat — about as mangy a thing as I'd ever seen — and coyote cap, and was warming his hands by the stove, talking to Gene Hardee, who stood beside him on his crutches, holding a tin cup. Both men looked at me. My eyes locked on the six-point badge pinned on Bitterroot's bib-front shirt.

"You a lawman?" I asked.

Bitterroot snorted. "I didn't steal this badge, boy. Can you read it? It says Deputy U.S. Marshal." He tapped the piece of shiny nickel. I'd pegged him for maybe a stock detective, but nothing like a federal peace officer.

Walter Butler sat in his bunk, saddle-stitching a pouch he'd been working on, but, noisy like he was prone to be, he put down his needles, deer hide, and sinew thread, and trained all his attention on me and Bitterroot Abbott. I hung my coat on the hanger, removed my scarf, hat, and gloves, working slowly, as unhasty as I could, but Bitterroot wasn't going nowhere, so at last I joined him and Gene Hardee at the stove.

"Hoped you was here," Bitterroot said.

"I ain't done nothing," I told him. I was defensive and defiant, yet truthful. I hadn't done a thing except work cattle and try to keep from freezing. I feared he wanted to arrest me for a robbery or murder. "I haven't been to Helena since . . . September . . . I reckon."

With a contemptuous snort, Bitterroot put

his coffee cup down. "This badge means I got jurisdiction not just in Helena, boy, but all across the district of Montana. I go wherever Marshal Kelley wants me to go, and I bring back whoever he sends me after. That's my job." He nodded, and reached inside a canvas bag he'd dropped by his feet, still talking. "Major MacDunn's letter of introduction proved mighty handy. The major thought I'd be a big service to him in a fight against Gow. 'Course, that war never panned out, but I'm beholden to the major. Pretty good job I got. Or so I thought, till I got caught in that God-awful blizzard. But, here I am, doing my job." He handed me a folded photograph, which he'd fetched out of his bag.

Slowly I pulled back the cold paper, careful not to rip it, and stared. Felt sick down to my stomach when I realized what I was looking at. A girl, younger than me. Hard to say with her face so cut up, yet I could tell she was dead when the picture got took.

Gene Hardee gasped, and swore at Bitterroot Abbott for showing such a thing, and Walter Butler jumped out of his bunk, and hurried over to see. When Gene started to jerk the photograph from my trembling fingers, Abbott snapped: "No, I want him to keep looking at it. I want him to remember it."

I dropped the picture to my side before Walter Butler got an eyeful. "What . . . I don't . . . what's this . . . got to do with me?" I looked at the lawman, but I couldn't get that girl out of my mind. Bloody, bashed up, folded hands holding a little old rag doll to her chest.

"Her name was Velna Oramo."

"I never heard of her. Never seen her before."

"I know that, boy. I just want you to remember her. She was on that train."

"What train?"

"The one derailed at the Little Blackfoot. Killed the engineer, killed the fireman, killed a drummer named Kelley, and it killed this here girl. Velna Oramo. Broke both of her mother's legs, not to mention her heart. Hurt a lot of other people, but it's the girl's death that got the Northern Pacific riled, got everyone in Helena wanting blood. She was nine years old."

"You should run the photographer who took that picture out of Helena," Gene Hardee said. "Takes one sick. . . ."

"He's no fiend," Bitterroot said. "Pictures like that make things personal, shows Montana what. . . ."

I'd heard enough. "I don't know this girl. I don't know anything about that accident. I. . . ."

"Wasn't no accident, Hawkins. That train was derailed on purpose."

Now, I understood. I dropped the photo. Waited for Bitterroot Abbott to finish.

"Your pard, John Henry Kenton was seen. Been identified. He stole a pickaxe from a railroad tool shed. Was overheard at the Crabtown Saloon saying he'd get even with the railroad. Said the N.P. never should have brought in barbed wire. Kenton's a murderer, Hawkins. A vicious, terrible murderer . . . four times over. A child killer. I'd hang him four times. I'd hang him forty times. He'll only hang once, but I'm after him, and you know me. I don't trust lawyers, and judges, and hangmen. And I figure you might know where he is." He pointed at the photograph by my dripping boots.

"Well?" he said.

I let his words sink in, but couldn't say anything. I'd close my eyes, and see that girl. I'd imagine the wreck. My stomach got all twisted.

Gene Hardee broke the silence. "Tommy O'Hallahan? Was he seen in Helena? At the Little Blackfoot?"

I wasn't sure I wanted to hear Bitterroot's

239

answer. "No," the gunman said. "Kenton was alone. Nobody knows what become of the other boy. Reckon folks would remember a face like his."

Abbott told us more. Kenton watched the wreck. The fireman lived long enough to describe him and the big sorrel horse he was riding. Other witnesses on the train and at the Crabtown Saloon gave a judge enough reason to issue a warrant for John Henry's arrest.

"The N.P.'s put up a five-hundred-dollar reward for Kenton," Abbott said, "and the residents of Helena added to that pile another five hundred. I aim to collect it. So I'm asking you once more, Hawkins. Where's Kenton?"

"Forget it, Abbott," Gene Hardee said. "Major MacDunn ordered Kenton off this range. Kenton's not here. Haven't seen him since Tristram Gow fired him. Jim Hawkins has been here, working hard. Boy helped save my hide when I busted my ankle in that first bad storm to hit us."

Abbott stared at me, but finally he nodded. "All right. The Bar DD was on my way. Figured I'd ride over to Gow's place."

"Gow wouldn't have anything to do with that!" Hardee pointed at the photograph on the floor.

"Well, I aim to collect that reward. Likely that dead girl's parents will offer even more than the thousand bucks already on Kenton's hide."

"It's just an arrest warrant, Abbott," Hardee said. "He hasn't been found guilty, yet."

"The man's guilty in my eyes. But no matter. What about the other one? The one-eyed kid, the boy who helped tear up all that wire by the river. He around?"

Holding my breath, I was thankful that Abbott looked at Hardee when he asked that question, and when Hardee answered.

"He's not here. You're welcome to stay, see for yourself. Ish, Melvin, and the rest of the boys should get back before dusk."

Abbott's eyes whipped back to me.

"What about you, Hawkins? You seen . . . ? I disremember his name."

"Tommy," I answered. "Tommy O'Hallahan. No, sir, I haven't seen him since. . . ." I shrugged. Not altogether a lie, I reasoned, and just hoped Walter Butler would keep his big mouth shut, prayed that Abbott wouldn't ask Walter anything. He didn't. Didn't even look at Walter Butler.

"All right." Abbott picked up the photograph by the puddle of snow melt, started to put it back in his sack, then walked over to my bunk, found my war bag, and shoved it inside, deep. "I'll let you keep this, boy," he said. "In case you see that Texas rawhide again. I might even be inclined to give you a bit of that reward if you tell me something I need to know. Something that helps me find Kenton."

"He's probably already in Canada," Hardee said.

"If he is, I'll find him," Abbott said. "Marshal Kelley's posting me at Great Falls, so if you hear anything about Kenton, you get word to me there. I'll find him wherever he is."

"Why'd you lie about Tommy?" I asked Gene Hardee after Bitterroot Abbott rode out of sight.

"Didn't lie," Hardee said with sad smile. "O'Hallahan ain't here. He's at the Sun River Cañon line shack." With his pocket knife, he carved off a piece of chewing tobacco, and put the quid in his mouth. "I'm not fond of Abbott," he said after a moment, "and I'll give O'Hallahan, after all he's been through, the benefit of a doubt. For now. But we'll need to keep our eyes open for Kenton. I'll ask O'Hallahan a few questions when he comes down for Christmas. But, Jim, if you run across Kenton, you light a shuck. Don't talk to him, just ride away. Man's gone loco."

I think it was the winter.

CHAPTER
TWENTY-FIVE

Christmas came and went, but Tommy never showed. That weighed heavy on poor Mrs. MacDunn. She fretted over Tommy about as much as I did, but Gene Hardee and Ish Fishtorn assured her that he likely lost track of the days. Wasn't no calendar at that line shack, or he simply had his hands full trying to keep the cattle out of the freezing river. Besides, the weather wasn't so inviting for a sixteen-year-old boy to ride those umpteen miles through snowdrifts and a miserable wind just for roasted goose and Sally Lunn bread. I hoped Tommy just wanted, needed, to be alone.

On Christmas night, it started snowing again, and it kept falling for two days. The wind wailed, and, when the storm finally broke, Gene Hardee sent Busted-Tooth Melvin up to the Sun River to check on Tommy. He said it was for Mrs. MacDunn's sake, but I suspect he worried over Tommy, too.

While we were waiting for Busted-Tooth Melvin's return, we got another visitor, and I didn't know what kind of welcome Major MacDunn would give Tristram Gow.

Never been much of a hand as a farrier, but Hardee had me shoeing horses with Old Man Woodruff. That's where I was when the rider come up. Upon hearing the major cussing, me and Woody put down our tools, and walked out of the barn, and into the wind.

"I warned you about setting foot on my land, Gow," Major MacDunn said.

Mr. Gow sat atop a big brown gelding, and he looked terrible, slumped in the saddle, and, when he removed his goggles — he had cut a little slit in them, protection from snowblindness so he could see — I saw how bloodshot his eyes were, how pale he was.

"Please . . . ," he began.

"Gow!" The major gripped the butt of the Bulldog revolver he'd stuck in his waist-band.

"Please." This time it was Mrs. MacDunn doing the begging.

The wind moaned through the cracks in the barn walls.

"It's Melvina," Mr. Gow said, choking back a cry of anguish.

The snow started falling, light at first, then steady. I remembered Camdan's ma, a frail, weak sort, recalled the time we'd spent at the 7-3 Connected, her fretting over the fact she might have to take to the root cellar, her always bothered by the constant wind.

"Come inside, Tristram," Mrs. MacDunn said, and the major barked a terrible oath, but Mrs. MacDunn ignored him, still speaking to Mr. Gow. "You look terrible."

"It's Melvina," he repeated. "She's run off."

Hearing that, Major MacDunn eased his hand from the revolver, took a deep breath, then spotted me and Woody eavesdropping on them. I thought he'd tear into us, but he just barked an order for us to tend to Mr. Gow's horse, so I come out, hesitant, and took the reins from Mr. Gow after he dismounted. Seeing him up close, I knew he'd been crying. Worrying over his wife. I wondered where she'd run off to. They walked into the house, and I led the heaving, cold brown gelding into the barn.

Old Man Woodruff sadly shook his head.

Lainie told me all about what was said inside the house.

Mr. Gow explained to the MacDunns that his wife had run off right before Christmas. He'd been looking for her, half crazy with worry.

"That poor woman," Mrs. MacDunn said.

"It's her mind," Mr. Gow said. "It's gone."

I think it was the winter.

He'd tried to deny it, Mr. Gow said, but Melvina Gow just couldn't cope with the terrible solitude, the wind, a sky so big it stretched toward eternity. Drove her mad. She lost all of her faculties. Took off in the buckboard. Camdan and his pa had been working the stock, with all the other hands, so nobody knew that Mrs. Gow had left the ranch house until much later.

"I have searched all over for her. Followed her trail. Lost it when the snow started." Mr. Gow kept shivering the whole time he talked, Lainie told me.

"How is Camdan?" Mrs. MacDunn asked.

"He's all right. Or was. Worried sick. Like me. I left him at the ranch. I didn't want him to find her in case. . . ." Mr. Gow started crying again. Took him five minutes before he could speak again, get control of himself.

"Gow," the major said, "your house is a day's ride from the Bar DD. In this weather. . . ."

"She had the buckboard," Mr. Gow said. "I found it five miles from here, the horse dead, frozen in the traces. So she had to be alive then. I'd hoped . . . maybe. . . ."

"Five miles might as well be fifty," the major said. "Or five hundred. A woman in her condition."

"There's always hope," Mr. Gow said, "and I had hoped . . . prayed . . . maybe. . . ."

"She isn't here," the major told him. "Where was your buckboard?"

"In a coulée. A mile from the dry creekbed. I just. . . ."

Mrs. MacDunn give him a big dose of brandy to help settle his nerves, and looked at Major MacDunn. Looked at him long and hard, the two of them never saying a word.

"You know she's dead," Major MacDunn told Mr. Gow bluntly, and Mrs. MacDunn and Lainie closed their eyes.

"I just have to find her, William," Mr. Gow said weakly. "Please."

"The weather's been warm," Mrs. Mac-Dunn said, looking at the major, her eyes hopeful. "Was warm. Maybe. . . ."

"She's dead," the major said.

"Father!" Lainie snapped.

"I have to find her," Mr. Gow said. He

248

started to rise, but his legs couldn't work, and he collapsed on the settee.

Another long silence followed. Slowly Major MacDunn rose from his leather chair, and grabbed his black greatcoat. "Your horse wouldn't carry you another mile," he said. "I'm not sure you can travel ten feet. I shall go."

With a determination that matched the major's bull-headedness, Mr. Gow pushed himself to his feet. "I must ride with you, William," he said firmly, but, when he spoke again, his voice faltered. "I have . . . must . . . she. . . ."

The major gave a nod of approval. "We will pick out a fresh mount for you. Come, Tristram. We shall find your wife."

They packed enough supplies for three days, bundled up for the weather, and rode out. We helped the major saddle two good horses, as well as a pack mule, and Old Man Woodruff volunteered to help look for Melvina Gow, but the major wouldn't hear of it.

"Be careful," Mrs. MacDunn told them, adding a prayer-like whisper. "Please."

The major just grunted.

I wonder if his heart had changed. Wondered why he was doing that, helping Tristram Gow. I wondered how Mr. Gow felt having to come to the Bar DD for help. No, Mr. Gow didn't have reservations about that. He was looking for his wife, or, more likely, his wife's body. He loved his wife. Would do anything for her. But the major? What was he thinking? Acting almost human. Maybe that had something to do with the winter, too, or maybe he was trying to prove something to Mrs. MacDunn. Make up for being such an ass. Well, I didn't know. Still can't be sure. Wasn't none of my affair, really. Just seemed strange, is all, unnatural. After all that had happened earlier in the year, no one between Great Falls and Helena ever would have expected to see Major MacDunn and Mr. Gow working together, almost acting like the friends they had been.

We watched the two men ride out together, ride until they disappeared in the falling snow.

The snow didn't let up, and the thermometer plummeted. Lainie, wrapped up in a heavy blanket, scarf, and three wool shirts, come over to the bunkhouse that night, even though it wasn't a Sunday, bringing some leftover bread for us boys to eat, and *Treasure Island* to read.

'Course, we'd finished the book several weeks earlier, but she still liked to bring it over, and we'd read some passages that we liked a bunch. She didn't have any interest in Mr. Stevenson's writing or Long John Silver, Squire Trelawney, Dr. Livesey, or that other Jim Hawkins. We sat by the stove, letting Walter Butler join us, while the other boys played poker and complained about the weather.

"Do you think Father is all right?" Lainie asked.

"Sure," I said. Had no reason to doubt it. He and Mr. Gow were well outfitted, and men didn't come any tougher or ornerier than Major MacDunn.

Meanwhile, we worked. Worked hard. Riding out in the snow, seeing nothing but white — and that's when we could see anything at all — moving to the creeks and rivers. Noon came and went without notice on those days, us pushing Aberdeen Angus and trail-thin longhorns up the hills.

"Keep them away from the river!" Ish Fishtorn kept yelling at me, until I snapped right back at him, pointing a gloved finger at our Bar DD beef. "Tell them! Not me!"

As soon as we got one bunch of cattle pushed back up the hills, away from the water, and herded them into what shelter

251

we could find in a coulée or cutbank, another group would wander down to the river's edge. Endless. I think I learned more cuss words that winter than I'd learned in all my life.

Cattle are stupid, but maybe cowboys are even dumber critters. Smart fellows wouldn't have been out in that weather, riding all day, hungry, mad, freezing. We had to keep the cattle from the river, or they'd wander out into the water, and, if the ice didn't hold them, or if they'd step into an air hole, they would get pulled under, drown or freeze to death. So we worked through snowdrifts, watching cattle so poor they could hardly stand. Saw steers who had worn the hide and hair to their hocks just pushing through frozen ice. The sight alone would have broken our hearts, had we not been so tired, so miserable. It's a miracle nobody else come down with frostbite or pneumonia. We worked until our lips cracked from the cold, until we could scarcely breathe.

No fiery furnace or smell of brimstone, but it was hell just the same. Hell on cattle. Hell on men. Hell on horses. I ruined Gray Boy that winter, riding through the snow, up and down those hills. By the time I got him back to the ranch one afternoon, I saw his legs, and grimaced. The icy crust had carved furrows up and down his legs. The blood had frozen, of course, and it's a wonder Gray Boy hadn't gone lame, but I knew I couldn't take him out in the blizzard again. Gray Boy was lucky. He got to winter in the barn.

I had no such luck.

The snow stopped, but the temperature kept falling, and the wind howled. The major didn't return that night — hadn't expected him to — or the next.

Busted-Tooth Melvin rode in — we'd all been hoping it was the major and Mr. Gow — and said he'd found Tommy O'Hallahan working and reading at the line shack. Working alone. No sign of John Henry Kenton. That was good news. We asked him if he'd seen any signs of the major, but he hadn't.

By then, I guess we were all worrying.

There's a reason I never like remembering Melvina Gow. A fine woman. But. . . .

I really like to remember her alive. But. . . .

Yeah, it was the winter.

That morning, I went outside to fork some hay into the corrals. Even before I fetched the pitchfork, Lainie had walked outside.

"Go inside," I told her. "You'll catch your death."

"Mother said to tell you to please ask Gene Hardee or Ish Fishtorn to come see her."

I threw hay into the corral. The horses were too cold to notice.

"I'll do it."

Figured she'd go back inside, but she just stayed, hunched over, steam rising from her mouth and nose, hands stuck way deep in her pockets.

"You think my father is all right?" she asked, trying not to sound scared.

"The major knows what he's doing."

I forked more hay.

"Mother's fretful."

"They had a pack mule loaded with food and stuff. Both of them know this country."

I walked around the pile of hay, jabbed the fork. I'll never forget the pinging sound of the vibrating tines as it hit something solid. Almost dropped the pitchfork onto the ground, it being so hard to get a good grip with my heavy gloves.

Forgetting that I was in the company of a lady, I let out a prime cuss word. I figured one of the boys had come up with a devilish prank. Seemed like just the gag Busted-Tooth Melvin or Ish Fishtorn would play on a greenhorn like me.

"Somebody put a rock. . . . Wait'll I get my hands on that reprobate."

I dropped to my knees, pulled back handfuls of ice-hardened hay. Lainie started giggling. Then she was screaming, and all the Bar DD hands came flying out the bunkhouse in an instant. Lainie's mother ran outside, and Lainie dashed into her arms.

I couldn't move.

Just sat there, staring at the frozen face of Mrs. Melvina Gow.

CHAPTER
TWENTY-SIX

You try to remember her one way, but it's hard. Every time I think I might be able to picture her as she was back at the 7-3 Connected, telling me about her fears, or talking about life in Scotland, or the time she rode up in the wagon to tell us about the range fire, how proud she was of her husband and son. . . . I want to see her that way, but then I can't recall nothing but her face in that hay pile. Unseeing, horrible eyes. Mouth open. Saliva frozen on her tongue and chin.

Miracle she'd lived as long as she had. She'd run off in nothing but her union suit. Well, I seem to recall someone saying she had a heavy coat and blanket, but she'd left those behind in the buckboard when she wrecked it in the coulée. Wonder where she thought she was going? To the railroad in Helena? Back to Scotland? To escape the incessant wind? We'll never know. Not in this lifetime. What drives a woman to flee her house in her unmentionables? What makes her hide from the bitter cold in a pile of hay? This country has driven a lot of homesteaders crazy. Cowboys, too. So lonely. So unforgiving.

We had no idea how long she'd been in the hay pile. She might have been there, long dead, when Mr. Gow rode up a few days before. If I'd fed the horses hay from that side of the pile, I might have found her earlier, but I didn't. Fate had dealt another hand.

"That poor, poor woman," Mrs. Mac-Dunn said. She'd come from the house, leaving Lainie trembling at the door. "Eugene, get her out of there, please."

On his crutches, Gene Hardee directed us, and the hired hands dragged Mrs. Gow's frozen body from the hay. We covered her in blankets, put her in the schoolhouse. Don't sound all that Christian, but the schoolhouse served as our Sunday prayer-meeting gathering, and we wasn't about to put her in the MacDunns' house, not with Lainie so shaken, and certainly Mrs. Gow deserved better than the barn. Old Man Woodruff said he'd fashion some kind of coffin, but Mrs. MacDunn said that would have to wait.

"We need to get word to my husband and Tristram." She sounded every bit like the major, taking command, barking an order that nobody dared challenge.

We found the snow-covered buckboard and dead horse in the coulée. It was pretty well hidden, practically covered by snowdrifts when we got there, so it's little wonder none of us Bar DD boys had come across it. Problem we had now was that cattle, wolves, snow, and wind had wiped out any sign of the major and Mr. Gow. So Ish Fishtorn sent us riding off in pairs, headed in different directions, hoping to cut a snow-covered trail.

I got stuck with Busted-Tooth Melvin. Not that I didn't care for Melvin or anything like that, it's just that I'd rather been riding with Ish Fishtorn or Gene Hardee, had Gene been able to ride.

Heading west, we kept silent, hunting for sign, yet having little luck. Snow glistened like millions of diamonds salted on the hilltops, with pristine, wave-like ridges. A huge gust would come up sudden-like, sending mists of snow scurrying across the ground. When we nooned, we didn't bother taking the bridles off our mounts. Wasn't no grass for them to eat, anyhow. Silently we ate jerky, our backs to the wind, and sipped water from our canteens, stamping our feet against the chill.

Finally Busted-Tooth Melvin said we'd best ride, so we went searching again.

We passed miserable Aberdeen Angus cattle — their black coats contrasting to the whiteness that stretched on forever. Toward midday, I turned a bit south, while Busted-Tooth Melvin rode north, so it was Melvin who found the trail. Hearing his pistol shot, I turned Crabtown around, and slogged through snow till I caught up with him. He'd dismounted, kneeling, looking toward the Sawtooths. When I reached him, he was rubbing his gloved hands.

"See that?"

First, I spotted nothing but snow, drifts of snow, ripples of snow, hills of snow. Yet, slowly, I could make out little mounds moving west. Snow had covered the tracks, but a good tracker could still make out the prints.

"Followin' somebody," Melvin said. He pointed west.

"Who?"

"Not Missus Gow, that's certain." He sprayed the snow with tobacco juice.

"Whoever they're trailin' was ridin' a horse," Melvin said.

That puzzled me. A moment later, I thought it might be Bitterroot Abbott, searching for John Henry. Next, it hit me that it could be John Henry himself. Before long, I knew certain sure it was John Henry. No reason to think that, but the feeling got stronger.

"Well." I filled my lungs with frigid air. "Well, why would the major and Mister Gow follow a horse? Missus Gow had no horse."

"I don't know," Melvin said. "Maybe they think the lady stole one of our'n. Maybe they think some stranger picked her up. Maybe they think Injuns taken her, run off with her. Folks don't think straight in this cold. What's certain, though, is Gow and the major rode after that rider."

"*If* it's the major and Mister Gow," I said. "Could be somebody else's trail."

Melvin spit again, and I'm lucky he didn't spray me. Likely he considered it, based on the look he gave me.

"Two horses and a pack animal," he said. "Now maybe somebody else fills that bill, ridin' on MacDunn range, in the dead of winter, trailin' a horse headin' west. So maybe it is somebody else. Who you reckon it might be?"

I apologized. Busted-Tooth Melvin accepted it with a grunt, and mounted his claybank.

"They're headin' toward Sun River Cañon," he said. "Could hold up at the line shack. Criminy, I just left that cabin."

"Maybe they think Tommy found Camdan's ma, and took her back to the cabin. Tommy could have been looking for cattle, come across her." I sounded like I wanted to convince myself of it.

Melvin shifted his chaw to the opposite cheek. "Maybe everybody in this country belongs in Bedlam." He studied the sky. "Can't tell exactly how old these tracks are, but it'll be dark before we could catch up with 'em. Maybe a day. Maybe even longer. Maybe never."

I nodded. "Be dark before one of us gets back to the ranch, too."

Melvin spit again. "You ride back, tell Gene what I've found. Send the rest of the boys after 'em. I'll follow this trail, and, if I lose it, I'll go to the line shack. You. . . ."

"I'd rather follow the tracks," I sang out, and watched Melvin study me. "I know the line shack and that country better," I reasoned. "I'm not sure I could find my way back to the ranch."

"Our tracks are a damned sight easier to follow than those," he said.

He stared. I stared back.

"I can't let you do that, boy." Melvin's head shook. "Can't let you ride off into that country. The major's wife would nail my hide to the barn if I were to let. . . ."

"I'm no kid," I fired back at him, and we got to staring at each other again.

We didn't say anything, but finally Melvin grunted. "Suit yourself. I got no hankerin' to see that line shack anytime soon. Besides, Tommy's your pard."

I let out a big sigh.

"Make for the cabin," Melvin said. "No matter where the tracks lead. If the major ain't there, you stay put. Don't go lookin'. That hard-rock Scotsman can take care of himself. You wait for us. Don't try to be no hero. You just fort up with Tommy, and we'll be there directly. If you meet the major and Gow riding back, you tell 'em what happened, and we'll find you." He reached behind him, opened one of his saddlebags, withdrew a small bundle wrapped in canvas, and handed it to me.

"Pine splinters," he said. "Soaked in coal oil. Come in handy if you need to start a fire."

I shoved them into my war bag.

"You be careful, Jim Hawkins."

"You, too," I said.

We shook hands before separating.

You ask why I wanted to ride after the major and Mr. Gow, but it really had nothing to do with them. Least, I don't think so. Then again, a boy don't think clearly when it's five degrees below zero, and it came close to that temperature that night. Yet I was pretty well clothed, and the skies cleared for the third night in a row — a rarity that winter, I guarantee you — and I found the Big Dipper, low in the horizon, just above the cañon. I knew if I kept riding toward it, I'd wind up close to Tommy's cabin. Close enough to find it, anyhow.

Where I expected to find John Henry Kenton.

Certainly I knew those tracks had to belong to my pard. Former pard, I mean. Former friend. My old mentor. I didn't think about the train he had derailed. I just thought about Bitterroot Abbott, who'd shoot John Henry before he'd ever bring him in alive to stand trial. Couldn't make myself believe than John Henry Kenton had killed that girl, and those other folks. Still, I knew I'd find him at the line shack, and I planned on warning him. Had I gone back to the ranch, sent Busted-Tooth Melvin west, well, Melvin might have gotten killed, or might have killed John Henry. More than likely Melvin would have waited for the rest of us when he saw John Henry was at the cabin, and then Ish Fishtorn and the boys would have captured John Henry.

John Henry would have hanged. I didn't want that.

'Course, somehow, riding all that night, I didn't think about the major and Mr. Gow. Didn't consider how they would reach the line shack long before me or the Bar DD riders, didn't consider what would happen if John Henry was at the cabin when those two men arrived. Like everyone kept saying — only I wasn't quite learning — people don't think right in that cold.

Sometime in the night, I no longer was following the tracks of Major MacDunn and Mr. Gow. Not sure I was following any tracks any more, and I'm just thankful Crabtown had a better nose and better eyes than mine. He knew his way. I'd fallen asleep, probably would have froze to death if Crabtown hadn't had a ton more sense than I ever had. A few hours past dawn, I reached the line shack, having ridden Crabtown all night. Don't know how long I'd been asleep in the saddle.

I jerked awake, saw the shack in front of

me, smelled smoke from the fireplace inside, felt Crabtown stomping his front hoofs. Wearily, as I swung down from the saddle into packed-down snow, the cabin door opened. A moment later, I recognized John Henry Kenton, and stared down the barrel of the Colt revolver he was pointing right at me.

CHAPTER
TWENTY-SEVEN

"Well, I'll be damned," John Henry said. "This place is busier than Booger Pete's bucket of blood in Mobeetie."

I expected him to look different, meaner, I guess, uglier, but he appeared the same, except for a few days' growth of beard, and I'd seen him like that plenty times before, especially when he'd been on a drunk. "You alone?" he asked.

"Yes."

As he holstered the revolver, Tommy came around the east side of the cabin from the makeshift horse shelter, carrying an armful of wood. When he saw me, he stopped in his tracks. The three of us just stood in the cold, looking at one another.

"Coffee's on." John Henry motioned inside, acting a whole lot friendlier than I'd expected him to be, than he had a right to be. "Some stale biscuits and cold bacon. Help yourself. You look a frazzle, kiddo. I'll see to your horse."

Too tired to protest, I watched him lead Crabtown away, and slowly followed Tommy into the cabin, closing the door behind me, watching him dump the wood by the fireplace.

Alone with Tommy, I got angry real quick. "That why you volunteered to be a line rider?" I hooked my thumb toward the door. "So John Henry could hide out here?"

He didn't answer, and I let all my weariness overtake my anger. I was just too tired to press him into a fight. He pulled off his sheepskin coat and one of his gloves, leaving the other on till he had poured me a cup of coffee. I took it, and collapsed in a rickety chair by the fireplace. Fell asleep before I'd even taken a sip.

When I woke, I almost toppled out of the chair, spilling the coffee all over my chaps. John Henry chuckled, and I knew I hadn't been dreaming. Had kind of hoped I'd wake up and find Tommy alone in the cabin, but there was John Henry Kenton, a murderer, relaxing on the stone hearth, hat pushed back on his head, long legs stretched out and crossed at the ankles, grinning. Didn't see Tommy.

"I threw your war bag and sougans over

yonder," said John Henry, motioning with his coffee cup. "What brings you here?"

Tommy walked back inside, and John Henry's smile faded. "You see anybody?" he asked Tommy, his voice suddenly demanding.

"No one," Tommy said. "Like Jim said, he's alone."

That seemed to satisfy John Henry, so he asked me again why I had ridden to Sun River Cañon. Instead of answering him, I fired a question at him and Tommy.

"Where's Major MacDunn?"

"MacDunn? What the devil does he . . . ?" John Henry set down his cup, nodding as he realized what I meant. "Oh, so that was MacDunn trailing me. Couldn't tell who it was."

"The major and Mister Gow," I said.

"Gow!" John Henry snapped. "What's he tracking me for? I ain't bothered him a bit."

"They're not after you," I said. "They're looking for Missus Gow."

"Well, she sure ain't here." John Henry laughed.

"I know that. She's dead."

A heavy silence fell over the cabin. John Henry's head dropped, and he mumbled something that sounded like: "She was a real nice lady."

Tommy asked: "What happened?"

So I told them about Mr. Gow riding up to the Bar DD, telling us how his wife had gone crazy, run away, about the major leaving with Mr. Gow to look for Mrs. Gow. About me and Lainie finding her, froze to death, eyes and mouth wide open, hidden in a pile of hay. About me and Busted-Tooth Melvin cutting the trail, and me heading here while Melvin rode back to tell the others.

"Then they'll be here," Tommy said. "Soon."

"Most likely," I answered.

Bitterly John Henry swore.

"What did you do to Major MacDunn and Mister Gow?" I asked John Henry, and he glared at me.

"Nothing," he said.

I turned back to Tommy, my ears starting to flame. "And you, pard. You never answered me. You decide to be a line rider just to keep John Henry safe?"

It was John Henry who answered. "Kiddo, I didn't know he was here. I figured somebody would be here, though I hoped nobody would. Hoped they'd have given up the notion of putting a man in this cabin for the winter, what with the weather. Hoped that I could warm up here. Wasn't sure where I was going, but then I seen the Big Dipper one night. Appeared to be ladling out some good, cold water from the Sun River. I was thirsty. Would have preferred rye whiskey, but a roof over my head and a warm fire would suit me just fine. The stars give me the notion to come here. Thought about heading up to Tie Camp Creek, but I suspect I wore out my welcome with them hackers. No, Tommy didn't know I was coming." He snorted, his face and voice turning bitter. "Don't think he was too happy to see me. After riding out on me in the middle of the night. Ironic, ain't it? Us three pals meeting together like this."

"Busted-Tooth Melvin rode here," I reminded Tommy.

"And left," Tommy answered, "before John Henry showed up."

My head snapped back toward John Henry.

"Where's Major MacDunn?" I challenged him. "He was trailing you. Thought you might be Missus Gow, I reckon. What have you done with him and Mister Gow?"

"Nothing!" John Henry exploded, clenching his fists, hovering over me. I thought he'd slap me to the floor. "I told you I didn't do nothing. Knew I was being followed, so I led them away from this shack, then doubled back."

"They'd come here," I said. "Eventually. Unless you killed them."

"They was alive when I last seen them," he said. "I ain't no murderer."

"You derailed that train!" When I spoke those words, I deliberately looked at Tommy, not at John Henry, because I just had to know. Tommy's face registered total shock, and that made me feel better. He hadn't been involved in the derailing of the Northern Pacific train. He wasn't a murderer.

But. . . .

But John Henry Kenton was. Just like Bitterroot Abbott said.

"That train," John Henry said, "was hauling barbed wire. That train is responsible for Tommy's face. I ain't ashamed."

"That was no freight," I said. "It was carrying people."

"My God," Tommy whispered.

"Wire!" John Henry barked. "The Northern Pacific. . . ."

"People!" I yelled. "Four of them are dead, including a nine-year-old girl!"

"Northern Pacific all the same!" he yelled.

"Murderer!" I screamed back.

He slapped me, but I didn't fall, and John Henry reached for his Colt, but didn't pull it from the holster. "That's why you come here, you liar," he said, trembling, his face a mask of hate, or rage. "You come looking for me. Same as Gow and MacDunn and all them law dogs! Gow's wife ain't dead. You just want me to believe that."

"No." My head shook weakly. "But I wish it was a lie. No, she's dead. Mister Gow and the major rode off looking for her. I came here . . . well . . . because we've been pards, John Henry, and I don't want to see you hang."

"So you knew I was here!" He slapped the other side of my face. Blood trickled from my split lip, but I looked John Henry in the eyes.

"I knew the major wasn't following Missus Gow," I said. "We rode out looking for them. They've been gone. . . ." Couldn't remember. I had lost track of the days.

Tommy cleared his throat, and started gathering all his heavy clothes. "I'll find Major MacDunn," he said. "I'll tell him about Missus Gow."

"The hell you will!" John Henry barked, but Tommy ignored him, went right on pulling on an extra shirt.

"I'll ride with you." I dabbed my split lip with my bandanna.

John Henry got his Colt halfway out of the holster, then angrily shoved it back.

"You two are the biggest fools in Montana." He jerked open the door. "You feel that wind? It's getting colder. Look at those skies."

"We're going," Tommy told him as he grabbed his overshoes. "You can stay here."

"Not for long," John Henry said. "Everyone has fixed that. Sure as hell I can't stay here. Riders from the Bar DD will be sure to come before long. MacDunn and Gow might turn back, seeking shelter. I ain't about to swing from some rope."

"They'll be coming," I agreed. "Least, someone will come, whether we go looking for the major or not. No matter if you kill us. Or not."

"Fools!" John Henry turned savagely. "It's started snowing again! You can't ride out of here. You can't leave . . . me!"

Without a word, Tommy pushed past him, and I followed.

Silently we saddled our horses in the pen, mounted, and eased the horses down the path between the cabin and a little grove of trees. John Henry stood at the edge of the cabin, shaking his head. Heavy flakes of snow already covered the brim and crown of his battered hat.

"This is plumb foolishness," he said.

Silently we rode right past him, but, when he yelled at us to stop, we obeyed, turning in our saddles, waiting.

I expected — well, I hoped — hoped he would tell us that he'd ride with us, but he just shook his head.

"I won't be here when you get back," he said. "*If* you get back."

Tommy nodded slightly, and looked down the slope toward the river.

"Hold up!" John Henry barked again, and let out a heavy sigh.

"You can't follow their trail. Snow's covered it by now."

He was right. I'd lost those tracks that night, and I didn't think even Busted-Tooth Melvin could pick up the trail by now.

"We'll find them," Tommy said.

John Henry swore again, and I thought he would go back inside, but he shook his head, staring at us. "Cross the river," he said at last, sounding defeated. "It's frozen solid, but be careful you don't step in an air hole. You'll come up by the old fence. Don't let your horses step on any wire buried under the snow. I led those following me north, up along that big mountain yonder." He pointed at Castle Reef. "Then I turned back when it got pitch black, figured they'd keep on north till they realized they'd lost my trail. Most likely, they'll make for the Seven-Three Connected. That's what you two kiddoes need to do. When you get on the other side of the mountain, turn east. Just ride north by east. North by east. Remember that. North by east. You'll likely find Gow and MacDunn, but, if you don't, keep on riding. North by east. When you hit Deep Creek, just follow it east. Stay on the creekbed, if you can. It'll keep you out of the wind. Just follow Deep Creek. That'll get you close enough to Gow's ranch to spit. I warrant you'll find them by the stove at Gow's ranch." He repeated the general directions. "You got that?"

"Yes," Tommy answered, and we rode off, hearing John Henry's final call.

"Good luck," he said.

We didn't reply.

The snow fell heavy, large, wet flakes, blanketing the horizon. Those clear skies were long gone, and me and Tommy rode in silence, following John Henry's directions.

I kept thinking we'd run into the major and Mr. Gow, heading back, giving up on finding the trail, and seeking shelter, and I wondered what we'd do. We'd have to go back to the line shack. The major would insist on it. Then what? I hoped John Henry would be gone.

The wind picked up, and the snow fell harder.

We stopped long enough to put on extra layers — the women's stockings over my sleeves, the face mask Melvin had made for me — and tied our bandannas over our hats, pulling the brims down. The snow kept falling. . . .

Harder.

Harder.

I quit thinking about John Henry, quit wondering about things like that, gave up hope on ever seeing the major and Mr. Gow because I could just barely see Tommy, and he was riding right beside me. The wind screamed. The snow blew sideways, no longer heavy, wet flakes, but frigid pieces of ice that slapped at us without mercy.

With a fury we had yet to see that winter, the storm raged. Our horses faltered. I yelled at Tommy, just a silhouette about to disappear, though he was no more than three feet from me. Yelled at him to dismount, that we had to turn back, find shelter. Yelled at him that we were about to die.

CHAPTER
TWENTY-EIGHT

The wind came from the north, terrible, brutal.

We turned back south — didn't have a choice — keeping Castle Reef to our right. At least, I prayed that big old rock face was to my right, prayed we were riding south. I couldn't see the mountain. Not a silhouette. Not a shadow. Nothing. Nothing but blinding snow.

Closing my eyes, I wondered if I had made a terrible mistake. Maybe we should have headed for the mountain. Maybe. . . . Too late now. Wasn't sure I could find it.

We moved with the wind, cold and miserable, and hearts filled with dread.

When Crabtown started faltering, I dismounted, holding the stiff reins, motioning for Tommy to do the same. For a moment we sheltered ourselves between the two horses, stamping our feet to get the blood flowing again.

"I'm sorry I missed Christmas," Tommy said.

I looked at him, worried. Peculiar thing to say. But I couldn't make out his face. With the shrieking wind, I could just barely hear his voice.

"It didn't amount to much," I told him. It hurt to talk.

I looked down. The snow was up to my boot tops. I bent low, checking Crabtown's feet, making sure the ice hadn't torn up his legs. No damage. No blood. Not yet, anyway. The horse snorted, and I rubbed his neck, the hair stiff, crusted with ice.

"Good boy," I whispered.

"I'm sorry I missed Christmas," Tommy said again. He sniffed.

I moved close to him. "Don't talk," I said. "Save your breath." I could make out his eyes now, wild, crazy eyes. Reminded me of the way John Henry had looked back in the line shack when he'd lost his temper. Kind of like that, but different. John Henry always seemed sure of himself. Tommy's eyes darted.

"I can't see anything!" he yelled.

I gripped his shoulder. "Listen to me," I said. I took a deep breath. Had to inhale with my mouth. Couldn't hardly get my nose to work. That was a mistake. It felt as if I'd filled my lungs with ice, that I'd frozen the insides. Hurt like blazes. I bent low, waiting for the pain to subside, slowly exhaling, then looking back up at Tommy.

The wind roared.

"We need to keep moving," I said. "I'll lead. You grab Crabtown's tail with your right hand, wrap the reins to your horse around your left. Keep your head low. Don't let go. Don't let go of the tail. Don't let go of the reins."

"How do you know we're going in the right direction?" he asked.

"The wind," I said. "Keep the wind at our backs. Storm's blowing in from the north. We'll keep going south."

"To where?" His voice ached with terror.

I had to keep my nerve, at least, sound like I knew what I was doing. If I broke down, we'd both die.

"Come on," I said.

He just stood there. I had to take his right arm, lift it, bring it to my horse. I watched him slowly grab a handful of tail. Then I pressed my hand around his, made sure he had a tight grip on that horsehair. Well, as tight as anyone could hold with stiff gloves. As I eased my way to the front of my horse, I tugged Crabtown's reins. Started walking. Pushing through mounds of ice that kept getting higher. Pushing on. Head down, whole body practically numb, moving with a purpose, although it seemed to take forever.

Every minute or so, I'd make sure Tommy was behind me. It was hard to see. It got harder to walk.

It got colder, and colder, and colder.

Concentration proved difficult. I had to remind myself how to walk. Right leg. Left leg. Right leg. Step. Step. Step. Stop. Look back. Right leg. Left leg. Forward. Forward.

God help me!

We had to rest frequently. Every fifteen minutes at first, but that soon shortened to ten minutes, then five. Before long, it wasn't minutes, but steps. Walking, though, seemed better than riding. The horses blocked some of the snow, ice, and wind. Being lower to the ground protected me and Tommy a little bit, and resting our two horses seemed prudent.

I lost track of time. Decided we'd better ride some. Thought the horses had rested enough, and the snow kept getting deeper, harder to slog through, and my feet felt so cold. I stopped, turned, made my way back to Tommy. He still held Crabtown's tail, but when I could make out what was behind him, I panicked.

"Tommy!"

He couldn't hear me. I stepped closer.

"Tommy!"

He looked up.

"Where's your horse?"

"Right here."

His left arm stretched out behind him, his hand in a frozen fist, but he held no reins. He pulled, like he was tugging on the reins, and stared at his empty hand, eventually comprehending that the reins had slipped through his fingers. Somewhere. How long ago?

I stumbled past him, a thousand thoughts racing through my mind. That horse meant our life. Now what? The wind blew me down. I found my feet, started, almost blindly, but stopped. Don't be a fool! I told myself. I couldn't see but a few feet in front of me. That horse could be twenty feet beyond that, or a thousand yards. That horse could have wandered off the trail — if I could even find a trail. Tommy's horse could be dead, covered by another drift. If I kept going, I might never find my way back to Tommy and Crabtown, so I staggered back to my pard and my horse.

"I'm sorry," Tommy said. "I thought I was holding. . . ." He looked again at his empty hand, flexing his fingers.

"It's all right," I lied. "Come here."

I helped him free his frozen hand from Crabtown's tail, led him to the side of my horse. I held the stirrup out, but Tommy couldn't lift his leg. "Grab the horn," I told him, and knelt, lifting his leg, putting his foot in the stirrup, boosting him up, grunting, lifting him into the saddle. He managed to swing his right leg over, found that stirrup on his own.

"Both hands on the horn." I made sure he followed my instructions. "Keep as low as you can." I wasn't sure he heard me.

"You. . . . ?" his lips mouthed. I couldn't hear him. I could barely see him.

My head shook. "Crabtown can't carry us both," I said.

With a soft prayer, I walked back, taking the point, pulling the reins, moving south. Or so I hoped.

On. And on.

Folks say it snowed for sixteen hours straight. How cold? I've heard twenty-two below zero. I've heard thirty below. I don't know. I walked until Crabtown stumbled, that poor horse's legs torn and bleeding from the shearing mounds of ice, then helped Tommy dismount. I didn't trust him to be able to hold onto my horse's tail, so we walked together, him to my left, me pulling Crabtown behind me, making sure every so often that I hadn't let those frozen reins slip out of my grasp.

We walked. Stumbled. Cried.

Tommy slipped, fell in deep snow, face first. I helped him up, clawed the ice from his good eye.

"Leave me," he said.

Shaking my head, I pulled him to his feet.

"I'll get a fire going," I said. "Find some wind block. Warm us." I went back to Crabtown, hoping those pine splinters soaked with coal oil would work just how Busted-Tooth Melvin told me they would. Wasn't sure I could find anything dry enough to burn. Wasn't sure I could even find any wood. I might just use the splinters, if only to warm our fingers for a minute.

My heart sank. I looked on one side of the saddle, then the other. The war bag had fallen off somewhere. No! I swore, bowed my head, remembering. John Henry had brought in the war bag and my sougans, tossed them in the corner of the line shack, and I had not thought to grab them when me and Tommy rode out to find Major MacDunn and Mr. Gow. I had no wood. No blankets. Nothing but the clothes on my back, a horse quickly going lame, and a weak friend.

I didn't even have matches. Lot of good those pine splinters would have done me.

"Keep walking," I told Tommy

"I can't," he said.

I didn't listen. I threaded his right arm through my left at the elbow, let my right hand grab Crabtown's reins, and we walked. Walked, the wind driving us, the storm's fury never dulling. Walked until Crabtown collapsed, blood frozen to his legs. This time, I couldn't get him up. I knelt by him, rubbing his neck. I wanted to tell him how sorry I was, wanted to put him out of his misery, but I had no gun. Couldn't even open the jackknife in my vest pocket. I left Crabtown, bridle, even that worn-out saddle I'd bought with those soap coupons what seemed like a thousand years ago. I locked arms with Tommy, and we abandoned Crabtown to be buried by snow and ice.

"Leave me," Tommy said.

Those were the last words spoken. For how long? I ain't rightly sure.

We couldn't talk. Not as cold as it got. Can hardly breathe when it's that cold. Head bent, I put my gloved right hand over my mouth and nose. That helped. Tommy done the same, using his left hand. We walked.

Right. Left. Right. Step. Step. Step. Stop. Rest. Right. Left. Forward. Forward. Keep the wind at our backs. Right. Left. Step. Step. Step. . . .

Please, God.

It had to be nigh dark. Hard to tell when you can't see the sun, can't see a thing except a raging blizzard, can hardly see two feet in front of you.

Tommy had fallen again. Now I had to drag him. I'd make, I don't know, five yards, then halt, trying to catch my breath, trying not to freeze the insides of my throat, my lungs. I'd drag him, stop, make sure he was still alive, then get as good a grip as I could on his coat, and pull, pull, pull.

The wind drove whirling snow into my face until I couldn't see. I dragged him, until I backed against something, and slid down, felt my coat slightly tear. Turning, I reached up blindly, grabbing, groping. My hand gripped . . . something . . . pulled myself up . . . stared closer.

The fence! Icicles snapped as I ran my gloves over that strand of Mr. Jacob Haish's S-shaped barbed wire. The fence. The stretch of fence that Tommy and John

Henry hadn't torn down. Only the top rows of wire hadn't been covered with snow, but I could make it out, the wire and a crooked cedar post.

I fell to my knees, jerked Tommy close, slapped his face until his eyes fluttered with faint recognition.

"The fence!" I whispered. I helped him to his feet, forced his hands on the top of the wire.

I pointed. Stepped in front of him, grabbed the wire with both hands. I took a step to my left, but stopped.

The wind wailed. I looked down the wire, but saw nothing but a world of white and gray. It was growing darker.

Which way?

The wind was at my back. Left was east. Wasn't it? I wasn't sure. Go east, I told myself, to the end of the fence. Left meant east. Sure. Wind's at my back. It hadn't changed directions. We hadn't walked in circles. Or had we?

Yeah, your mind don't think straight. Not in twenty below.

Left. I nodded, trying to convince myself. Left meant a chance at life. Right meant death.

It had to be.

I took a tentative step. Made myself keep

going. Kept looking back to see Tommy.

"I can't feel my legs," he told me.

I grabbed his hand with my right, moving down, pulling him, praying.

I reached out for the wire, found nothing, and fell. The fence had ended. Tommy collapsed on top of me, and I thought we'd both be buried in three feet of snow. That barbed wire had gotten us this far. The rest had to be up to me and Tommy. And God.

That's right. Infidel cowhand like me . . . praying.

Tommy was unconscious. Maybe dead. I couldn't be certain. I slapped him, but he wouldn't come around, so I dragged him. Dragged and rested. Dragged. We went down the bank, and I slipped, rolling to the Sun River. I clawed my way out of the snowbank, blundered to Tommy, lifted him again. I hadn't guessed wrong. We had to be close to the cabin. I felt the ice of the frozen river under my feet.

Going down the embankment was one thing, but now I had to climb up. Had to pull Tommy. We'd get part way up, then slide down. Or roll down. My whole body felt encased in ice. I'd given up trying to wipe the frozen snow off my clothes. Moved like I weighed a thousand pounds. The scary thing was that I started feeling hot. Sweating. That was terribly dangerous. Deadly. If that sweat froze, I'd die. So would Tommy.

I grabbed Tommy's shoulders, began pulling dead weight. My boots found a ledge, and we moved sideways for a few yards, then I backed into a fallen tree. I used it as a ladder, somehow, working slowly up the bank. Reached the clearing. Felt the wind.

It was dark.

Dragging Tommy, I moved. Bouncing off trees now, finding some shelter, though not much, from the wind.

I had to be close to the cabin. But how close?

I turned, saw nothing, and screamed: "Help!" My lungs burned. Why? Wasted breath. Nobody was there. Nobody could hear me. Where was the line shack?

I started, stopped, cursed my stupidity. I had almost forgotten Tommy. Mind's going, and my strength ebbed. It was a miracle I'd gotten this far, but wouldn't that be ironic? To die, so close to a cabin that I couldn't see. I could hear Busted-Tooth Melvin joking about that come spring. Joking over my grave. If anyone found our bodies.

Grabbing Tommy again, I pulled, heaved, backed up. My back pressed against something solid. Too flat for a tree. Boulder? I turned, hands groping, feeling, flattening, running from side to side.

The cabin!

No. But it was a structure. Privy. The privy. But I couldn't get my bearings. Which way to the shack? Which way to life? I moved past the outhouse, the wind blasting me, and my side pressed against something. Firm. Small. A rope.

Rope!

A rope, tied to a post next to the privy's door, stretching out into the white darkness. Before he had left the cabin, I thought, John Henry must have secured the rope, to use it as a handhold, to find his way from the line shack to the privy. Follow the rope, and I'd find the cabin. My heart pounded. I grabbed Tommy again, one hand holding the rope, one hand lugging Tommy. Moving, half crawling, backing, biting, praying, struggling through the snow. Knowing that we were going to live.

And . . . just like that . . . all those hopes died.

The rope ended, but not at the cabin. It had been tied to a corral post. The rope had been put up as a guide from the privy to the corral. To check on the horses. There had to be another rope, then, to the cabin, but I knew I could never find it. Didn't have the strength to pull Tommy from the horse shelter to the cabin. I barely had enough strength to open the gate.

I left it open, somehow managed to get Tommy underneath the lean-to. I fell on frozen hay, brought Tommy close to me. A horse snorted. I must be dreaming. There couldn't be anyone at the cabin. John Henry had to be long gone. No, one of Tommy's string. Or could it be? Someone had put that rope up. It hadn't been there before we left. I tried to stand, but couldn't. Didn't have an ounce of strength left in me. Weakly I leaned against Tommy, letting our body heat warm us, if only slightly.

Stay awake, I told myself. Go to sleep and you'll die.

It didn't matter, though. I was dead anyway. I pictured Mrs. Gow. Wondered if my face would look so horrible when someone discovered my body.

CHAPTER
TWENTY-NINE

The smell of coffee lured me out of a bottomless sleep. My eyes opened, and, for a moment, I saw nothing but raging torrents of snowflakes, felt myself rocking in the wind. The vision, or nightmare, passed, and a roof came into focus. Then John Henry's face. Then nothing.

When I next awoke again, I saw the dim glow of a lantern, surrounded by darkness. Above the moaning wind, I made out what sounded like humming. Certainly not angels singing. I tried to move, but couldn't, and felt a presence hovering over me again. A voice spoke, and the lantern revealed a face. John Henry Kenton's face. He said something. At least, his lips moved, but I didn't hear. I felt his hand on my forehead, cool. Cool. It felt so fine. I was burning up.

On fire. After being so awful cold, now I raged from heat. Sweat streamed down my cheeks. Hot. Blazing hot. I must be in hell.

"Rest," his mouth moved, and I slept again.

Don't know how long I slept, really. At some point, I was lucid enough to ask John Henry, or what at that time I figured for an apparition of John Henry Kenton, about Tommy.

"He's all right," the ghost spoke. Sounded just like John Henry. This time I had heard him, too. Not just read his lips. This time I didn't feel so infernally hot.

I woke again. No longer sweating, or chilled. Things became clear. I lay on a cot in the line shack. My mouth was parched, and I tried to throw off the heavy woolen blanket, but didn't have the energy. Boots thudded, and John Henry sat beside me.

"It stopped snowing," he said.

"Water," I begged.

He left, returned, lifted my head, and let me drink from his canteen.

"Not too much," he said, pulling the canteen from me. I sank back on the bed.

"Hey," I suddenly blurted out, "I'm alive."

He smiled, a sad smile, and I slept again.

"Can you eat?" John Henry asked as he propped my head up, using my sougans as a pillow.

"A little," I answered. Staring across the room, I spotted Tommy O'Hallahan lying on that bearskin rug by the fireplace, kept looking at him until I was certain the blankets covering him were rising and falling over his chest and stomach. Yeah, he was breathing. He was alive.

So was I.

John Henry brought a bowl, sat beside me. He give me a hard look.

"Jim," he said, "I want you to listen to me. Before you eat." His Adam's apple bobbed. "Listen. I had to take off the pinky and the tips of two fingers on your left hand."

I jerked my hand up, stared, not quite believing.

"But. . . ." I turned back to John Henry. "I still feel them."

"I had to do it, Jim," he said. "You're lucky that's all you lost."

My hand dropped on the blanket. I looked again, flexing the fingers I had left. I could still feel those digits. Sometimes, even today, I still look down, can't believe they're gone.

"Hey, kiddo," he said, smiling again. "How many cowboys you know with all their fingers?" He held up his hand, wiggling his pointer, showing the missing top that he'd lost on a dally down in Texas. "I always looked at it as a medal of honor. It ain't so bad. It's your left hand, and that little finger ain't much use to anybody. You can still rope. Still ride."

I started to cry. He put the bowl on the floor, pressed his hand on my shoulder.

"You're alive, Jim. Don't you forget that."

After swallowing, I wiped my eyes. "Tommy?" I asked suddenly. "Is he all right?"

Slowly John Henry bowed his head. "Some toes on both feet. Both boots was filled with snow. Had to cut the things off, they was frozen so. Cut off his boots, I mean. He lost two toes on both his feet, but he'll be fine. Boy's tougher than a cob. So are you. Couple of toes and fingers is all you lost, when by all rights you both should be dead. Now, you best eat." He brought up the bowl again.

The next day, I got out of bed, poured myself a cup of weak coffee. We didn't have much in the way of supplies. The line shack had been stocked for one cowhand, not three. I sat staring at the bloody ends of my fingers. It would take some getting used to, but I figured John Henry was right. I was alive. Wasn't sure how, but I was alive.

"How'd you find us?" I asked John Henry when he came inside with an armful of wood.

"Went out to check on my horse," he said. He stoked the fire, tossed on a chunk of wood, the water from the snow sizzling, and leaned over Tommy.

"How you doing?" John Henry asked.

"All right," Tommy said sleepily. "Where's Jim?"

"Right over yonder," John Henry answered.

I wet my cracked lips.

"My feet feel funny, John Henry," Tommy said in a far-off voice, and my head dropped in shame.

Wearing a pair of moccasins that John Henry fetched from his saddlebags, Tommy limped over to the table the next afternoon — first time he had gotten out of bed, and collapsed in a chair.

When I looked down, Tommy's fist slammed on the table, almost knocking over my cup.

"Don't you pity me, Jim!" he snapped. "I'll be just fine!"

My head bobbed slightly, and John Henry sat between us.

"I thought you'd be long gone from here,"

Tommy told him.

"Was my intention," John Henry said. "Got caught in the storm, too. Rode back. Problem was, I'd taken Tommy's string with me. Figured the Bar DD owed me that much. Took the string and the mule. Lost them in the storm. We only got one horse." He shook his head. "Never thought I'd see you boys again."

"I'm glad you did," I told him.

He laughed.

"It snowed for ten days. Practically all the first day, then stopped, then started up again. More snow out yonder than most folks would see in thirty lifetimes. Somebody brought a thermometer, a real good one, here, and nailed it on the tree right outside the door. It was minus forty-seven degrees one night. I went out to bring in some wood. You two were in fits then. Wasn't sure you'd come around. Went out, and on a whim, I held out the lantern and read the thermometer. Might have gotten colder after that, but I wasn't curious about how cold it was after I seen that. Couldn't get much colder than that anyhow. At least, not by that thermometer. It don't go no lower than fifty below." He sipped coffee, and shook his head. "I bet the company that made that thermometer never even thought it would ever get that cold."

"What's it like now?" I asked.

"Cold. Windy. Cloudy."

"What do we do?" Tommy asked.

"We wait," John Henry said.

Which is what we done. Waiting for that Black Wind to free Montana. John Henry fashioned a rough limb into a cane for Tommy, and he got to where he could move around the cabin pretty good. Limping badly, of course, but far from crippled. I mostly forgot all about my missing digits.

I remember opening the door, just looking in amazement at a world of white. When I wondered about the cattle, John Henry snorted.

"What cattle?" he said.

I closed the door.

The Chinook came. Boy, did it ever come, a gale wind roaring from the west off Castle Reef, blowing like a furnace at fifty or sixty miles an hour.

John Henry had shoveled out a path to the privy and corral, and a little patio area outside. Not that we had any need to step out of the line shack for most of January, but we did when the Chinook came. We ran out — ran out without our shirts — laughing at the warmth. Forgetting all of our troubles. We were alive. Melting snow glistened like diamonds. I threw a ball of snow at Tommy, and he slipped, giggling, falling into the wet snow. For a minute, I felt bad, expecting Tommy to lash out in rage, but he pulled himself to his mangled feet, still laughing, shaking his head. He even joked about it.

"You wouldn't be able to do that if I had all my toes."

"What do you mean?" I said. "I done that with my left hand." I'd actually used my right. "Don't have all my fingers, and still knocked you on your fanny!"

He made a big snowball, and returned the favor.

We played for a few minutes, then went inside. And things went all wrong.

"Let's play some poker, kiddoes," John Henry said. "One of you boys must have some playing cards."

I went to frying up some corn mush, while John Henry searched for a deck. He opened my war bag, and I started to tell him I didn't have no cards, but then he pulled out that picture. The picture I'd forgotten. I'd forgotten everything.

As John Henry stared at it, his face went all white, and he turned.

"What kind of sick . . . ?" He shook the photograph Bitterroot Abbott had stuck in that canvas sack. "What is this?"

Grabbing his cane, Tommy limped over, took a quick glance at the photograph. He looked at me, his face hard, worried, sickened.

"Her name," I said slowly, walking away from the cast-iron skillet, "was Velna Oramo." Surprised I could even recall her name.

Somehow, we'd forgotten all about what had happened. I'd blocked out everything before the blizzard: John Henry derailing the N.P. train at Little Blackfoot Crossing. Killing that nine-year-old girl and three men. John Henry posted for murder. Lord, I had even forgotten why me and Tommy had gone out before the blizzard hit.

"Major MacDunn," I whispered. I closed my eyes.

"What happened to this girl, boy?" John Henry snapped. "What fiend carries a picture of a dead kid?"

With a heavy sigh, I opened my eyes.

"She was on the Northern Pacific you derailed, John Henry," I said. Only it sounded like somebody else was talking. A voice far away, deep in a well. But it was me. I was telling John Henry. I was remembering everything. "She was one of the four people you killed." I walked to the door, opened it, feeling the Chinook's warmth. Again, I softly spoke the names of Major MacDunn and Mr. Gow.

Behind me, paper crumpled. When I turned back, John Henry was standing by the fireplace, watching the photograph burn. Tommy limped over to me.

"Funny," he said.

I stared at him. Funny? What could be funny?

"That wire," he said after a moment. "Barbed wire."

Bewildered, I shook my head.

"It wound up saving our lives."

I didn't think about that. Instead, I stepped back to the table.

John Henry just stared at the orange flames. Seemed to have forgotten all about us.

"I wonder," I began, "if the major and Mister Gow . . . ?"

"They're all right," Tommy said as he hobbled back to me. "Likely made it back to Mister Gow's ranch before the blizzard even hit."

"No."

We turned to face John Henry. He gathered his coat and gloves, pulled them on despite the blowing Chinook, and picked up his bridle. "I lied to you boys," he said softly. "I didn't send MacDunn and Gow north. I led them into the cañon, then doubled back. Told you otherwise, hoping you'd keep on riding to Gow's ranch, and you likely would have, if the blizzard hadn't hit. No, that storm caught Gow and Mac-Dunn in the cañon."

He lifted the saddle to his shoulder.

"Where are you going?" Tommy asked.

"To fetch them home."

"You can't do that," I said. "They're dead."

John Henry lowered the saddle, put his hand on Tommy's shoulder. "There's one horse. You can't ride. Not yet, anyway." He turned to me. "I'll go. I'll find their bodies. I'll bring them back." He swallowed, and his voice almost cracked. "Least I can do."

Adamantly I shook my head. "You can't go, John Henry. I won't let you. That Chinook's melting a lot of snow. In that cañon, you might get caught in an avalanche. Besides, if they're dead, they . . . well . . . you couldn't find no bodies till spring. Maybe summer."

"Maybe never," Tommy said.

John Henry just lifted the saddle. "I'm proud of you. . . ." He grinned. "No, I can't

301

call you-all kiddoes no more. You're grown men. I know I promised you that old six-shooter of mine, but, well, I traded it for a bottle of rye a while back. I'll buy you both a new one, though, come summer." His face hardened. "I'm going. You stay put. If the weather stays warm, the Bar DD will send somebody here. You'll be fine. So will I." He gave a little chuckle. "A little snow ain't gonna kill John Henry Kenton."

CHAPTER
THIRTY

We never. . . .

Well. . . .

It was a hard winter. Worst winter I ever saw. Just as quickly as it had blown in, the Chinook died. Did nothing but start melting the snow, and, when the next storm hit that night, it turned that slush into solid ice.

That night, we sat by the fireplace, never talking, staring at the door, hearing the wind, the creaking cabin. Felt like the gusts would just tear that line shack apart. We kept waiting for John Henry Kenton to walk in.

'Course, he didn't.

I wonder if he planned it that way. Nah, couldn't have. He didn't know another blizzard would blow in. Impossible. Storm probably surprised him as much as it surprised everybody else. Or did it?

No point in wondering. Don't matter.

Maybe it was better that way. John Henry doing something good, maybe something right. Better than swinging from the gallows.

Well, that's the way January and February went. It would warm for a little bit, then another storm came blasting in from the north. Me and Tommy were stranded. Without any horses. Wasn't no game around, either, but in February I come across one of those black heifers that had wandered up from the river to the horse pen, where it had finally died. That fed us some.

Tommy got to walking pretty good, almost wore holes in the soles of his moccasins, and my left hand healed. Got to where I became used to not having all my fingers. So, we went through the rest of the winter together, but we seldom talked. Just worked at staying alive.

One morning, I stepped outside, feeling the strong gust of another Chinook, and stood staring at a clear sky. Felt like forever since I'd seen the sun. Then I heard the whinny of a horse, and moved through the melting snow to the clearing, looking below at the Sun River, hoping to see John Henry Kenton riding out. Four riders came, one leading a pack mule, another pulling a string of four horses, but they came from the east, not the cañon.

Blinking, I stepped back, unbelieving. A minute later, I whipped off my hat, waving it over my head till my arm hurt. The horses plodded on, but one of the riders responded by signaling me with a black hat. Instantly I turned, slipped on a patch of ice, climbed back to my feet, and yelled: "Tommy!"

"Riders!" I shouted when he appeared in the doorway, and he walked out slowly, picking his way gently, and we stood together, waiting.

Gene Hardee, his busted ankle healed, just stared at us. We couldn't find the words, either. He turned to Ish Fishtorn, who grinned, and broke the silence.

"You two boys need a shave," he said.

I rubbed my face with the back of my hand.

One of the men I didn't know, but he was riding a 7-3 Connected horse, and the string behind him was all 7-3 Connected geldings, too. I knew the last rider, the one pulling the mule. Camdan Gow tried to talk, but it took him a while. He was afraid, I know. Afraid of the answer. He kept looking past me and Tommy, staring at the shack, waiting, hoping, praying that someone would walk out.

"Is . . . ?" His eyes landed on me. "Is anyone . . . ?"

My sad reply broke Camdan's heart, but he had grown up a lot that winter, too. He tightened his lips, nodded, and swung from the saddle.

"What happened?" Gene Hardee asked.

"We thought you were dead," Ish added.

Took some explaining, which we did in the cabin. I'm not sure we told them everything. Not sure we even remembered it. I forgot a lot, just blacked out whole chunks, but later, over the years, bits and pieces would come back to me. Fill in the holes. Some I was glad to know, happy to remember. Others . . . well . . . I wish I didn't recollect everything.

It hadn't just been hell on the Sun River range. Cattle wandered down the streets of Great Falls, Ish told us, starving, eating the saplings the citizens had planted that summer in hopes of making their town more beautiful. Eating garbage. Dying in the streets. Dying in the doorways. Dying. Dying. Dying.

The temperature reached sixty-three below zero somewhere. Gene Hardee couldn't remember the exact place, and we told him how cold it had gotten here.

"How's Lainie?" I asked.

"She'll be finer than frog's hair cut eight ways," Ish Fishtorn said, "when she sees you two boys."

Camdan stood in the doorway, staring toward Sun River Cañon. "We need to go," he said. "Need to find. . . ." His head dropped.

He was right, of course. We needed to go fetch his pa and Major MacDunn back home. Fetch John Henry home, too.

Figuring the last of winter had blowed itself out, we left the line shack, putting two horses in the corral. The 7-3 Connected rider, a man named Ryan, led the pack mule. 'Course, me and Tommy had no saddles, so we rode bareback.

Into the cañon.

Oh, we didn't get far, not that first day. Ice and falling snow forced us back, so we returned to the cabin, and waited. Our first plan had been to split up, and fire a shot if we found anything, but Gene Hardee rethought that when he saw all the snow still packed atop the mountain. He wasn't about to fire no shot. Start an avalanche. Bury all of us.

The weather held, and, two days later, we rode back into the cañon. Quiet, I remember, except for the wind, the sound of dripping water. The sound of hoofs pushing through snow and mud.

That night we camped. Saying nothing. Wondering. Hoping.

Hackers come down the following morning, hauling a load of timber on sleds. When they learned what we was doing, they joined us, and we started covering the woods, and the wall of the cañon. Working cautiously. Using poles to feel our way through the snowdrifts.

It was Tommy who found them.

Had to be toward midday when me and Ish Fishtorn rode out of a thicket, and spied him on the far side of the river, standing in front of a cutbank, waving his hat over his head with his right hand, his left clutching the hackamore to the horse he'd borrowed. We eased our mounts across the riverbed.

Tommy pointed. "They're around the bend," he said.

"Who?" I asked.

"The major," he said softly. "Gow."

My chin fell against my chest. I made myself look up. "John Henry?"

Tommy shook his head. "He's not there," he said.

"Wait here," Ish said, and he rode off to fetch the others.

I climbed from my horse, and me and Tommy stood together, silent. A coyote yipped, and I thought I even heard a bird sing out.

The hackers arrived, rolling smokes or lighting pipes. Nobody spoke. Nobody went around the bend to see for themselves. Maybe ten or twenty minutes later, Gene Hardee rode up, followed by Ish, the 7-3 Connected hired hand, and Camdan Gow.

The hackers agreed to hold our horses, give us our privacy, but said we could use the sled to cart those bodies to the line shack. Gene Hardee led us into the brush, but he turned before he had gotten to the path, icy still as it was well-shaded, and asked Camdan if he was up to this, said he could stay behind with the hackers if he wanted to. Wasn't no shame in that. A good thing, the 7-3 Connected man said. "Remember your pa as he was alive."

"I'll go," Camdan said. "I have to go."

Gene Hardee give a little nod. "You're a man now, Camdan," he said, and he looked over Camdan's shoulder at me and Tommy. "You're all men."

We walked along the side of the cañon, feeling our way gently, hands pressed against the limestone rocks or shrubs to keep our balance.

Never found the horses or pack mule, not even the bones. Tommy pointed to the shelter. Gene went in first, then called for Camdan. We give him a few minutes before ducking underneath the overhand.

"So peaceful," the man called Ryan whispered.

Wolves hadn't gotten to Major MacDunn or Mr. Gow. I feared they might have. In fact, it looked like they'd just made camp there. Pretty good place, I thought. I bet Major MacDunn had carried some pine splinters soaked in coal oil, had gotten a fire going underneath that overhang. They'd stayed by the fire, their backs to the wall, huddling together when the last piece of wood had burned.

"What are those?" The man named Ryan pointed, and I saw the red hand prints.

"Indian sign," Ish Fishtorn answered.

"Wonder who made them," Ryan said.

"Shut up," Gene Hardee snapped. He walked over to Tommy, asked him in a low voice about John Henry Kenton, but Tommy just shook his head.

"We'll keep looking," Gene Hardee said. He glanced over his shoulder, saw Camdan Gow kneeling, staring at the two dead men.

"I'll look," Tommy said. "I'm the line rider here. I'm supposed to be here till spring. That's my job."

"There's nothing for you to do here, Tommy," Gene Hardee said. He suddenly sounded so old. "The Bar DD's finished. Hell, I think half of the ranches in Montana are finished. Maybe all of them."

"Can't be that bad," Ish Fishtorn said, but he didn't sound certain.

"I'll stay," Tommy said. "Leave me a horse and a saddle."

"You can barely walk," Hardee said. "Even Frank Raleigh quit after. . . ."

"I'm not Raleigh. I'm staying," Tommy said. "I can walk just fine. And I earn my pay. You take care of. . . ." His head tilted.

There wasn't no arguing with Tommy. Gene Hardee understood that.

"Well," he said, turning away, looking back at Camdan. "We need to get Camdan home. Need to get his pa . . . get the major . . . home." Sadly he shook his head.

I was looking at Tommy, but he give me a nod. "I'll be all right," he said. "I'll see you back at the ranch. When it's really spring."

That's how things would be. Tommy

would stay at the line shack, searching for cattle. If any cattle were still alive. Searching for John Henry. Well, searching for his body.

Camdan's head was bowed, and his hands were clasped, as he prayed. We took off our hats, waiting, staring.

It struck me then, seeing Major MacDunn and Mr. Gow sitting there, together, leaning against one another, right hands clasped together.

Like they were shaking hands when they died.

CHAPTER
THIRTY-ONE

Riding tired horses, heading southeast, they crest another hill, and Henry Lancaster recognizes the land, knows he and his grandfather will be home soon. As they head down the easy slope, Henry gives Jim Hawkins a sideways glance. The old man hasn't spoken much since they left Sun River Cañon, but Henry understands there must be more to his story. Too many questions that haven't been answered, details left unexplained, and he knows he must have those answers before they're back home.

"So," he begins, "you married Grandma."

With a harrumph, *Jim Hawkins spits to his side. "Appears obvious, don't it?"*

The boy blushes, stares ahead.

Silence. He feels his ears starting to turn red, and he realizes he does have a healthy dose of Hawkins blood shooting through his veins, but a gust of wind cools his embarrass-

ment and anger, and his grandfather apologizes.

"I didn't mean to be smart, boy. I know you want more to my tale. I don't know if I got the words."

Silence.

Then: "Don't know what Lainie ever saw in me," Hawkins says with a mirthless chuckle, "but we've had some good years together. Some bad times, but mostly good."

"Did she ever . . . talk about . . . your friend, Tommy O'Hallahan?"

Another hill. A calf bawls. Henry sees a tree atop a hill just a few hundred yards away. Beyond that is home.

"Sure. We both talked about Tommy. Still do, often enough. Well, maybe not often, but I'll bring him up, or she'll mention something he did or said or read. I don't think she's regretful none, and I ain't jealous. Things burn themselves out sometimes. That's what happened between Tommy and your grandma. Not that she or Tommy knew anything. Hell, we was all kids." Jim Hawkins smiles, remembering. "Kiddoes."

He turns, one hand holding the reins, the other gripping the cantle. "I know you think I'm Methuselah, boy, but I ain't but fifty years old. That's how old the major was when he died. This country, though, ages you fast.

Except Lainie."

Henry swallows. He feels impatient, but he wants to be careful. "Can you tell me what happened?" he begins.

"Thought I told you."

"Not everything," Henry says.

Silence.

"What happened to Tommy?" That's not the real question, though. He chews his bottom lip. A dog barks in the distance. Smoke serpentines from a chimney into the cloudy sky.

"What happened to John Henry Kenton?"

No answer. Hobo, their hound, has raced over the hill, barking, its tail zipping back and forth with happiness. Henry grins at the dog, but looks back, eyes hopeful, at his grandfather.

"Things change," Jim Hawkins says at last. "Between people. Like Tommy and Lainie. Like the major and Mister Gow. Like between me and Tommy. And John Henry. Things change. People change." He sighs. "Times change."

He opens up . . . one last time.

Spring, 1887

[The] day of vast herds is coming to a close . . . but instead of one man or one company owning 10,000, one hundred men will own them. The day of great losses, too, will then be over.

Honest cattlemen concede this. It is inevitable.

— Laramie Daily Boomerang,
August 6, 1887

CHAPTER
THIRTY-TWO

Everything changed with the winter of '86 and '87. We thought the cold and snow would go on forever, but the Chinooks came, and spring soon followed. It always comes — spring, I mean — and with it blooms new hope. 'Course, it took me a long while to realize that.

Somehow, the 7-3 Connected fared better than most ranches, maybe because Tristram Gow's herds weren't fresh off the trail like a lot of Major MacDunn's beef, and he leased some range up along the Milk River that wasn't so overgrazed. Overall, the Gow spread reported a loss of twenty percent. Lucky. Only a boy, Camdan Gow went back to his spread, and took Ish Fishtorn with him, started building his daddy's ranch up again. Built it up by cutting it back, fencing in pasture, reducing his herds, growing hay. I don't reckon he was the first to change, to see how things must change, but he was one of them. Before long, a body would be hard pressed to tell a sodbuster and a cowboy apart.

But, I remember the afternoon when Camdan Gow rode up to the Bar DD. It was later that year, and he told Mrs. Mac-Dunn he'd come back to school. Well, that teacher broke down crying, but she toughened herself up, and led us into that broken-down schoolhouse. That time, I was glad to go. Glad for her. I kept right on going to school, although Mrs. MacDunn would be the first to tell you that I never bettered myself as a student. Tried, but I wasn't cut out for schooling like Tommy. Or Camdan. Or Walter Butler. I was a cowboy. And Blaire MacDunn was a teacher, and a mother to us all.

The board of directors in Aberdeen liquidated the Dee & Don Rivers Land and Cattle Company, Incorporated, but offered to pay return passage to Scotland for Mrs. MacDunn and Lainie. They wrote Sir Alistair Shaw back, thanking them for the offer, but letting them know they'd stay. Montana was their home. So Mrs. MacDunn went right on teaching at that schoolhouse till it burned down in '91, then moved up to Great Falls, and taught there till she went practically blind. Even then, she'd help teach anybody who'd stop by her cottage, and I expect she'd still be at if the influenza hadn't called her to Glory a while back.

The influenza also claimed Ish Fishtorn and that Fort Shaw girl he up and married. Killed a lot of good men, women, and children. It's always something, ain't it? If not the winter, then the drought. If not the floods, then the locusts. I remember one thing my pa told me. He said: "Farming starts with a seed and a prayer. That's the way it always has been, and that's the way it always will be." That's one thing my pa said that made sense to me, and I reckon it holds true for ranching, too. Ranching starts with a cow and a prayer.

Life's always a struggle here.

Gene Hardee stayed with us as foreman for a few more years, as Lainie and me tried to make our own ranch work. Finally Hardee got a better offer, took over an operation on the Tongue River, till he got too stove up to work. Don't know whatever became of him, or a lot of the other boys that rode for the Bar DD. Bitterroot Abbott got killed in Helena a year or two later. Not in a gunfight. No, nothing like that. Poor fellow got drunk, fell down some stairs in Helena, and broke his neck. Walter Butler? He's a dentist, got a fancy office in Butte.

Doing well, though he lives in Butte. Never cottoned to that town none.

There's some who say that the hard winter wasn't so bad, that not as many cattle died as all the newspapers and ranchers and ranch managers and boards of directors reported. We heard the same things down in Texas after that January blizzard, too. Oh, I suspect some folks killed off book counts and not actual herd counts, but it wasn't no lie. Dead cattle were everywhere, worse than it had been in Texas. Thousands drifted to the frozen rivers, and got swallowed down the air holes. They'd get pushed into the water from behind, cattle being so stupid, and drown or freeze. Wolves got plenty, and the winter got plenty of wolves.

A lie? The Bar DD went under. Even Teddy Roosevelt had had enough, eventually gave up his Dakota ranch. Other ranches — even the big Swan Company in Wyoming — filed for bankruptcy. Bankruptcy. Liquidation. Them's big words. Lots of other ranchers just quit. They were beaten. Losses reached sixty percent, seventy-five percent, ninety percent.

Mrs. MacDunn and Lainie, though, had no quit in them. They were stayers, like Camdan Gow. Hadn't been for Lainie and her ma, I would have likely drawn my time

320

along with Busted-Tooth Melvin, Old Man Woodruff, rode south.

Instead, spring found me where I'd been early in '86, only not in Texas, but on the Sun River range, doing what no respectable cowboy would want to be caught dead doing.

When Tommy O'Hallahan loped up, I stepped away from the dead heifer I was skinning, wiped the mud and grime off my gloves, tried to shoe away the horde of flies. Tommy rode right up to me on Midnight Beauty, war bag looped around the horn, other possibles — including his books — strapped to his sougans behind the cantle.

For a moment, we just looked at each other, unable to speak. Finally I broke the silence.

"When did you get back from the line shack?"

"This morning."

"Did you . . . ?" I couldn't finish.

He shook his head. "No sign."

"Maybe he made it," I said hopefully. "You know what he always said. 'A little snow ain't gonna kill John Henry Kenton.' "

"You're probably right. He's in Canada by now. Where there's no barbed wire."

I smiled. 'Course, we both knew better.

"I'm leaving, Jim," he said, and my stomach twisted in a knot. "Rode over to say good bye."

"Lainie know you're leaving?" I asked.

"She does."

A warm wind blew, but I felt so cold.

Tommy cleared his throat. "I can never repay you for all you did for me, Jim. You saved my life up there. You didn't have to do that. You've always been a man to ride the river with. You've always been a friend. I wish I'd been a better friend to you."

I had to take a deep breath. It didn't help none. Tears still welled in my eyes, and one rolled down Tommy's cheek.

"Where you bound?" I made myself ask.

"I don't know. Judith Basin maybe. Miles City. Dakota. I'm too much like. . . ." He hesitated, had to cough again. "Too much like John Henry. Too set in my ways."

"Too smart for your own good," I joshed him.

"Not smart enough." He smiled weakly. "You're the smart one, Jim. You've always been smarter."

He leaned down, we shook hands. His grip was firm. "See you when I see you," I told him, and he pulled his hat low, and rode east.

I watched him ride. I knew I'd never see him again.

Never did. You remember last year when we went to Great Falls? Remember that artist we ran into? Charlie Russell? Yeah, he's made a mighty big name for himself with his paintings, but he's still a heathen cowboy like most of us. He told me he worked on the Judith that summer of '87 with a young one-eyed cowhand, said he was a pretty good cowboy, and that must have been Tommy. The way I figure it, Tommy spent that season around Utica, then kept moving. Looking for what I knew, and expect he knew, too, that he'd never find.

Those days were over. The open range done for. But it wasn't the end. I knew that as soon as Tommy rode off. For me, for most of us cowhands and stock growers in Montana, those of us who had the grit to stick it out, it was a new beginning.

Slogging through the mud, I made my way slowly to the coffee fire down the hillside, out of the wind, where Lainie and Mrs. MacDunn were fixing some chow for the boys. Lainie looked up at me, and I could tell she'd been crying, too, but she gave me her best smile, saying: "We're going to be all right, Jim Hawkins."

She handed me a cup of coffee, and, as I sipped it, I walked back up the hill, silently, and looked across the gently, rolling plains, walked a few yards away to the edge of a muddy coulée. Lainie was right, though maybe I didn't know it then. Woman's always right. On that April morning in 1887, I saw a coulée filled with dead cattle. Later, however, I'd see the spring turn wet, and the grass grow strong. I'd see a land so fresh, so alive, so rich.

And Lainie would see it with me.

AUTHOR'S NOTE

Two pieces of art I first saw as a high school student inspired this novel: W. H. D. Koerner's "Hard Winter," painted in 1932, and a drawing by a Montana cowboy named Charles Marion Russell. To answer a rancher's question of how many cattle had been lost, Russell made a watercolor sketch on a piece of cardboard of a starving, dying steer and a hungry wolf. "Waiting for a Chinook" became synonymous with the disastrous winter of 1886–87.

Although almost all of the characters in this novel are fictitious, much of this novel is true. The events of the drift fence in Texas, the blizzard of January 7, 1886, and what Texas ranchers came to call "The Big Die-Up" are based on fact. Likewise are the natural challenges Montana stock raisers faced and fought over the following year: a harsh drought, overgrazing, grass fires, all of which led to the disastrous winter of

1886–87.

Cowboy "Teddy Blue" Abbott estimated that sixty percent of all cattle in Montana were dead by March 15, 1887. Only forty percent of Granville Stuart's stock on the DHS Ranch survived, and other ranchers in Montana, Wyoming, and the Dakotas reported devastating losses. On the Tongue River range, the Kempton and Tusler Cattle Company reported a loss of about ninety percent. The sprawling Swan Land and Cattle Company in Wyoming, the Dickey Brothers Ranch in the Little Missouri River Valley, and the Niobrara Land and Cattle Company declared bankruptcy. Theodore Roosevelt said he lost approximately sixty percent of his cattle. By 1890, Roosevelt, now living full time in New York, abandoned his Elkhorn Ranch. Roosevelt's 1886 appearance in Helena, Montana, by the way, is my own invention, although part of his speech regarding the future of the open range comes from an 1886 article in the *Chicago Tribune* that the *Yellowstone Journal* reprinted. By no means did the hard winter of 1886–87 end the cowboy way of life, but it certainly marked a closure to the open range era.

Happy Jack Feder put my son and me up for a few days at his cabin in Lewis & Clark

National Forest — the location became the site of the Bar DD line camp at Sun River Cañon — while I was researching this novel in the summer of 2008. He also gave me a tour through the cowboy country of Augusta, Choteau (where Pulitzer Prize-winning novelist A. B. Guthrie Jr. called home), and Fort Shaw. I'm deeply thankful to Happy for his hospitality. My son thinks Happy's one of the best marshmallow roasters on the Front Range.

Many thanks also go to Laura Rotegard, superintendent at the Grant-Kohrs Ranch National Historic Site in Deer Lodge, Montana, for granting me access to the archives, showing me around the ranch, answering all my questions, and, in general, putting up with a nuisance like me; Donnie Sexton at Travel Montana; Forrest Fenn of Santa Fe, New Mexico; the Santa Fe and Vista Grande public libraries; the Wyoming and New Mexico state archives; Montana Historical Society and its excellent museum in Helena; Panhandle-Plains Historical Museum in Canyon, Texas; and Devil's Rope & Route 66 Museum in McLean, Texas.

I found much material from the following books: *Alex Swan and the Swan Companies* (Arthur H. Clark Company, 2006) by Lawrence M. Woods; *Cattle-Raising on the Plains of North America* (University of Oklahoma Press, 1964) by Walter Baron von Ritchofen; *Conrad Kohrs: An Autobiography* (Platen Press, 1977) edited by Conrad Kohrs Warren; *Cowboy Culture: A History of Five Centuries* (Alfred A. Knopf, 1981) by David Dary; *Forty Years on the Frontier* (Arthur H. Clark, 1925) by Granville Stuart, edited by Paul C. Phillips; *Montana: A History of Two Centuries,* Revised Edition (University of Washington Press, 1991) by Michael P. Malone, Richard B. Roeder, and William L. Lang; *Montana: High, Wide, and Handsome* (Yale University Press, 1943) by Joseph Kinsey Howard; *Reminiscences of a Ranchman* (University of Nebraska Press, 1962) by Edgar Beecher Bronson; and *We Pointed Them North: Recollections of a Cowpuncher* (University of Oklahoma Press, 1954) by E. C. "Teddy Blue" Abbott.

Those sources are great starting points to learn the true story of Montana's Hard Winter of 1886–87.

Johnny D. Boggs
Santa Fe, New Mexico

ABOUT THE AUTHOR

Johnny D. Boggs has worked cattle, shot rapids in a canoe, hiked across mountains and deserts, traipsed around ghost towns, and spent hours poring over microfilm in library archives — all in the name of finding a good story. He's also one of the few Western writers to have won three Spur Awards from Western Writers of America (for his novels, *Camp Ford,* in 2006, and *Doubtful Cañon,* in 2008, and his short story, "A Piano at Dead Man's Crossing", in 2002) and the Western Heritage Wrangler Award from the National Cowboy and Western Heritage Museum (for his novel, *Spark on the Prairie: The Trial of the Kiowa Chiefs,* in 2004). A native of South Carolina, Boggs spent almost fifteen years in Texas as a journalist at the *Dallas Times Herald* and *Fort Worth Star-Telegram* before moving to New Mexico in 1998 to concentrate full time on his novels. Author of dozens of published short stories, he has also written for more than fifty newspapers and magazines, and is a frequent contributor to *Boys' Life, New Mexico Magazine, Persimmon Hill,* and *True West.* His Western novels cover a wide range. *The Lonesome Chisholm Trail* (Five Star Westerns, 2000) is an authentic cattle-drive story, while *Lonely Trumpet* (Five Star Westerns, 2002) is an historical novel about the first black graduate of West Point. *The Despoilers* (Five Star Westerns, 2002) and *Ghost Legion* (Five Star Westerns, 2005) are set in the Carolina backcountry during the Revolutionary War. *The Big Fifty* (Five Star Westerns, 2003) chronicles the slaughter of buffalo on the southern plains in the 1870s, while *East of the Border* (Five Star Westerns, 2004) is a comedy about the theatrical offerings of Buffalo Bill Cody, Wild Bill Hickok, and Texas Jack Omohundro, and *Camp Ford* (Five Star Westerns, 2005) tells about a Civil War baseball game between Union prisoners of war and Confederate guards. "Boggs's narrative voice captures the old-fashioned style of the past," *Publishers Weekly* said, and *Booklist* called him "among the best Western writers at work today." Boggs lives with his wife Lisa and son Jack in Santa Fe. His website is www.johnnydboggs.com.